MILT CHANEY'S TAVERN

Don L. McCorkle

DEDICATION

To Linda – wish you were here !

CONTENTS

ACKNOWLEDGMENTS

Many thanks to Louise Pettus, Professor Emerita, Winthrop University, who has made numerous contributions to local history in and around Lancaster County, SC. Also thanks to her brother Lindsay Pettus for his knowledgeable contributions and the use of his painting of the Milt Chaney Tavern for the cover.

Many thanks to Wanda Mayhugh for her editing skills and spot on suggestions to make the book much more easily read and grammatically correct – and, her encouragement.

PREFACE

I first heard sensational tales from my grade school friend Ronnie Ashley about the old shack just south of where I grew up in an area of Lancaster County, SC, called Indian Land. I finally read Louise Pettus's historical account of the era when the building was an inn on the much traveled road from Camden, SC, to Salisbury, NC.

It seems there were suspicions about the proprietor, Milt Chaney, in the 1850s, murdering travelers who had the misfortune of stopping at his inn for what they thought would be a good night's rest. Evidently, Milt Chaney was intelligent enough to cover his tracks- if he was indeed guilty of any such crimes- so that no one ever collected enough evidence to bring charges against him; however, he did make the fatal mistake of being caught, convicted, and hanged for slave stealing. Questions about him having accomplices with his alleged dastardly deeds were never answered.

The main story follows Thaddeus O'Donnell, a railroad foreman, and his crew leader, "Big George" McAfee, who initially uncover bodies in 1888 while digging near the old inn. The two decide they owe it to themselves and others to solve the mystery of the bodies.

Carter Bradshaw, the grandson of a cotton broker whose fate was sealed when unavoidable circumstances brought him to the inn for a night's rest, is determined to resolve the mystery of his grandfather's disappearance in 1854, over 30 years earlier.

Like Carter, Barron Haile, the Lancaster County Sheriff in 1888, becomes obsessed with solving the mystery of the tavern bodies because he wants to vindicate his grandfather who was sheriff at the time of Chaney's alleged crimes.

Readers must pay attention to the dates of each chapter because of time shifts during the story. The personalities of friends, including some locals, were used in portraying the characters.

The conclusion is – well, just as any good story should be – bittersweet.

As for the number of real bodies – that secret died along with Milt Chaney and perhaps others who knew of his alleged evil deeds.

<u>Reminder</u>:   Please be careful   to pay close attention to the time frame of each chapter. The chapters are   relative to particular years. Thanks , and I hope you enjoy.

CHAPTER ONE

The Legend of the Tavern
What the Old Folks Said
1980s

"The big man, with beady evil eyes, holding a rope in his hand peeps through a well-placed hole in the wall into the darkened room where the weary unsuspecting soon-to-be victim lies in the comfort of his bed. A sliver of light from the almost full moon piercing through a small gap in the boarded shutters is just enough to let his peering eyes see when the moment for the gruesome task which is about to take place is just right. Fate has brought the exhausted traveler here for what he hopes will be a well-deserved night's rest, but fate is about to give a final twist to this man's last journey on this earth.

The premeditated yank of the rope is swift and sure. The trap door in the ceiling springs open and the heavy anvil plunges downward to do its dastardly deed. It finds its target. The pain is excruciating, but only for a moment; the final breath is gone. Another unsuspecting victim has met his fate.

The victim's valuables are quickly and methodically fleeced from him. He is stripped to his undergarments. His mostly naked body is grabbed by the huge man and hoisted as a sack of grain would be. It is taken to an already well-prepared grave so cleverly placed no one is ever likely to stumble upon it.

The slightly waning moon gives glow to the knee deep haze which has lifted from the hollows near the creek close by and has crept over the whole of the area. The shadowy figure is brokenly silhouetted by the beams of light seeping into the secret, cleverly hidden burial place. The first shovel of red clay finds its way onto the still warm body. The shoveling, feverishly but quietly as possible, continues until the ground is level once again.

The vines are methodically spread over this latest victim's final resting place. The gruesome part of the night's work has been done.

The horses, wagons, contents, and anything which might be evidence this person ever visited this horrific venue are prepared and moved to sites elsewhere by the light of the moon. It all happened between midnight and before the slaves at the nearby plantations had begun to stir for their day's duties.

When morning dawned to the next day's world, it was as though nothing unusual at all ever happened the night before in this forsaken place. The unsuspecting weary traveler vanished from the earth and left no trace. Those who once knew of him will wonder his whereabouts forever!!"

◆

The tales of Mr. Jimmy Wilson, "Grandpa Jim" as he is called by those who endear him, are many.

When he has gathered the children - and anyone else who will listen - around him, he pushes up his black-rimmed glasses, leans forward, clears his throat, and begins his tale. He wants the children to know the legend which has been passed on by his father and those who lived in the era of the strange dark happenings at the small tavern which still stands in the Osceola Community in the panhandle of Lancaster County, South Carolina. After all, it was Mr. Jimmy's father and his partner Madison Gordon who sold lumber to Milt Chaney to build what was to become the infamous tavern.

The vines, underbrush, and small trees have since covered the old outpost, but its ghostly remnants were still visible in the year 2000. The old shack had survived the War Between the States, foul weather, and all the other hardships it could have known. Maybe the lingering spirits saw to it they had a *resting place.*

◆

Has another perfect crime of a sinister mastermind been committed?

Has it been an act of a lone perpetrator or has it been a conspiratorial effort to un-mercilessly kill and rob an unsuspecting stranger?

Is this the real story of what happened to the unfortunate visitors as they met an untimely fate? No one knows for sure how the plan was carried out. But the facts are for certain - when the railroad came through in 1887-1888, and they were digging the hill away at Osceola to lay track, they found bodies near the old tavern. It is not known for sure how many bodies were uncovered. What finally became of the bodies is not known either, nor is the actual identity of all who had unknowingly chosen to make this their last stop on their earthly journey.

The travelers had vanished in this wilderness and the circumstances had proven to be the perfect setting to allow it all to take place with impunity. If anyone at the time actually knew who was involved and what had happened to the victims and their belongings, they never told - at least no one *outside their wicked ring.* They took their secrets with them to their *final resting place... if they are indeed resting?*

♦

The old timers also had a *saying for the children,* "When the big rounded rocks near Osceola hear the train whistles blow, they all spin around."

As the puzzled children looked on with amazement in their young faces, the old timers would laugh and say, "Rocks can't hear." Then they all would laugh.

But there was no laughter when the old timers spoke of the tavern of Milt Chaney. If anything did move when the train whistle blew, *it was most likely the spirits of those who were snatched away by the vile acts of this evil man... and possibly a band of others who aided him.*

Footnote: There is a rumor about two men searching for gold on the old Chaney site in the 1950s. They supposedly found an old anvil hidden under a huge rock. There was a large part of the horn (sharp point) missing. It looked as though it had been broken. They found nothing else suspicious or worth noting on or around the old place.

CHAPTER TWO

The Railroad
The Bodies
1887-1888

Big George McAfee stood 6 feet 5 inches tall and weighed 275 pounds. Most of the time, Big George was dressed in his overalls with a sweatshirt resembling old *long johns* underneath. He kept a tattered red bandana in his back pocket to wipe away the sweat from his brow. His raggedy old straw hat had seen better days, but it provided adequate relief from the sun.

In sheer strength, there were no equals known anywhere about. Most people who had ever seen Big George work a team of mules swore to the fact of his ability to grab the mules' harnesses and pull them out of a predicament if the mules got bogged down and could pull no more. Not once had anyone ever known Big George McAfee to mistreat an animal.

◆

The railroad construction team worked in groups of twelve men. They set up their large, dull-white, thick canvas tents along the route they were clearing and otherwise preparing so the tracks could be laid. The tents gave them shelter from the storms of summer and from the cold of winter. It was a home away from home for some workers, and for others, it *was* their home.

They also tended the needs of their mules and horses. Their appearance as a group of vagabonds belied their ability to get work done in an orderly fashion. The working day was from sunrise to sundown with a break for the noon meal and time out for watering and feeding the animals. The meals were cooked on site and usually consisted of dried meat, beans, rice, and whatever *special treat* they might find along the way. The cook also tended the campsite while the workers were out during the day.

The men were congenial in spite of their different ethnicities. Such things did not matter to them. All were hard workers and it was about a job and nothing else.

Big George always worked the lead, whether it was cutting trees and brush or pan work. He was well-respected and had been placed in charge of the crew during those times even though African Americans were usually not put into such leadership roles. Because of his prowess, he was the exception.

◆

Nothing angered Big George and there was nothing earthly he feared. He had been brought up as a small boy on a plantation when slavery still existed. Now, the awful War Between the States was well past and the South was once again prospering because of the new economic opportunities which existed. Building railroads was one of those opportunities and it generated businesses throughout the nation. The industrialization of the South was helping to change the purely agrarian society into one which many people could leave the fields for a steady paying job in a factory or a mill.

This particular railroad line now being constructed from Chester County, South Carolina, to Monroe, North Carolina, would connect the agriculturally rich areas to other rail lines to ship goods north to the factories or to the seaports in the south. On the return, manufactured goods could be brought back for sale. It would also be a source of transportation for those who chose this new method of travel.

Earlier attempts to use the creeks and waterways for trade and transportation had not met with much success.

The attempt to place canals to get past the rocks and raging waters at Landsford, just south of Rock Hill, (west of Osceola) had failed, and the idea of shipping goods and traveling along the Catawba River was eventually abandoned. The insurmountable obstacle of the falls just down the river a few miles should have made any project moot from the start; such was not the case. In fact, a town which grew up there later was named Great Falls in respect for the sudden elevation change in the river. However, the spread of the railroads eventually did make the canal ideas obsolete. The futility of the efforts of those who thought canals were a grand idea is displayed in a few abandoned stone locks near the Catawba River's edge at Landsford.

◆

It was late in the afternoon when the crew first came to an area suitable for making their camp. The same area would later become the village of Osceola. As a matter of fact, as the railroad was being constructed, the village was being surveyed by a different survey party. The name had already been decided. It was chosen in honor of a Native American Chieftain from Florida who had taken his warriors north through this region to help White settlers fight other Native Americans.

The railroad survey crews had left a trail where the area was to be graded. Trees and brush had been cut, cleared, and the stumps removed, and now there would need to be considerable pan work to cut away dirt from high places and fill low places with it. It seemed simple enough, but it would take a long while to accomplish. The rolling hills made for a perfect setup, cut a high place, fill a low place. They would also need wagon loads of rocks hauled in to keep the areas around the creek beds from washing away once they were filled with dirt.

While they were scouting around for an area to set up the camp in preparation for work on the site, Big George and Thaddeus O'Donnel (the crew foreman) had come across the spring which had been used for decades at *the big rock* near the old north-south Continental Road. They would need water, natural shelter for the animals, and a generally favorable site. This certainly fit the bill. They would be there for several days. Osceola Hill, as they now called it, was a formidable task to cut through. It was, and still remains today, an exceptionally high place on the geological landscape of the area.

They had dreaded encountering such a massive hill since they had first known about it, but it had to be done. *Perhaps the dread was also for other reasons unbeknown and certainly unimagined at the time.*

◆

As he looked about the soon-to-be campsite, Big George's keen eyes noticed a crop of pretty yellow flowers along with other vegetation growing near a stand of trees. To him, it was a problem. The vegetation posed a danger to the animals. As soon as the remainder of the crew was there, he would be sure to tell them, "Don't lets them animals eats on any of the pretty yeller flowers or dem berry bushes right over there. If'n they don't dies outright, theys be sick for a long time!"

He had spotted yellow jessamine along with pokeweed. It was a good crop, too. If ingested, the pokeweed could be fatal to the animals. He had learned about poisonous plants from his daddy. There were also other plants there. Big George didn't know what they were, which was unusual.

Osceola Hill!!!

"Big George, we gottah cut through this dreaded hill and our cut will be purty wide. We'll need to fill with it in both directions, both east and west. We'll also need to get a bunch of rock as we move on eastward," Thaddeus O'Donnell instructed Big George. There was still a hint of an Irish accent although he had been in the new country for a long while. His family had emigrated from Ireland years before when he was a small boy. He himself was a sizable man with the ruggedness of an Irish fighter etched into his being. His reddish hair glistened in the sunlight.

"Big George, we're gonna need to do a lot of digging here. We're gonna start down the center where the rail will go and I suspect by the time we get down to grade, we'll be digging near the old shack yonder on the one side and near the big rock on the other. Don't think we'll hav' ta' move either. The banks are gonna be purty steep and it's gonna be a pain, big man, it's gonna be tough. Aye, but like we always do, we'll git it done," O'Donnell said with confidence.

"You might want to scout around to see just how hard it's gonna be as we widen out the dig. I'll need to know so I can plan how long we'll be here so I can get supplies sent in," O'Donnell continued.

"Yes, sir, cap'n," was the quick response from Big George. "I'se might pokes around a while this aftanoon while the mens bringing in the rest of the animals and wagons."

At his first opportunity, Big George did set out to do as he had promised. He picked up a good stick he might use for killing a Copperhead snake if he came across one. He had dealt with snakes before. He knew it was rare for deadly poisonous snakes such as the rattlers to be around these parts. Nevertheless, he was exceptionally cautious as he approached a patch of honeysuckle vines which were flourishing along with other growth.

As he was poking around to test the soil, Big George glanced in the direction of the old shack and got an ominous feeling. He brushed it aside and went on with his work. Strangely, he felt compelled to stare once again at the old vine covered ruins. He felt an almost threatening sensation in the whole of his body, but he continued his work.

There might have been a good reason for a person with Big George's gift of premonition to feel the attraction to the old building. Unknown to Big George, Thaddeus O'Donnell, and any of the people who were working on the railroad was the history of the old building. The rundown old shack was none other than the infamous *Milt Chaney's Tavern* which had served travelers in the late 1840s through the mid-1850s.

The old inn's service to travelers had come to an abrupt end after its owner had been hanged in 1856. However, rumors abounded... he had not been hanged for his most serious crimes. Unfortunately, no one could ever find any evidence of these alleged crimes. Then again, no one had ever suspected someone might hide evidence so close to his own business. Maybe the *secret hiding place* was the genius of it all. *No one would suspect and no one ever looked!!*

No one ever investigated after Milt Chaney was gone either. Maybe the thick vines which now covered the entire building kept people away. The faint-of-heart were never going to go there and the area was still sparsely populated even after the War Between the States. Also, the road had been relocated. It had been a place forgotten, perhaps on purpose. Maybe it was all rumors anyway or just stories to tell around campfires to create fear in the night. *Maybe?*

♦

When Big George looked further about, he could see

places with rock where he was not fond of digging. "Mighty poor land," he thought. Big George prodded the edge of the vines with his stick and felt what might be good dirt. If he cleaned back the vines for a few feet or so, he could tell for sure. He got his sling and ax and made a few chops. He reached down, grabbed a handful of vines, and tore them out by the roots. It looked more promising than he had originally thought. "This jus might be an all right place for digging," he said to himself.

But it would be tomorrow or later. There was still setting up camp, tending to the animals, supper to be fed, and bedding down for the night. It was coming up on a full moon, and the creatures would be moving about, and the horses and mules might be restless, so he wanted to get an early start on the night's chores.

He also wanted to give the area where he would have to dig a better look in the morning and see if he still felt the same as he did when he first saw it. He would be up right after dawn to check it out. Rising early had stuck with him from the time he was a boy when he and his father would do the early morning chores on the master's plantation.

The Eerie Night

Two days had passed and significant progress on cutting the hill at Osceola had been realized. The days had been especially tiring. Maybe they had pushed a little too hard.

The horses and mules had been fed, cared for, and

everything seemed well, except for Big George. There was uneasiness in the calm, a kind of foreboding. The *ominous feeling* had returned. He felt it throughout his body. It was stronger than the first time he had experienced it. *What was this all about?* Big George was uneasy – to say the least.

As a youngster, he had seen these similar feelings in his parents and the elders. It always resulted in something bad happening shortly thereafter. God had given him such an exceptional ability, too. He knew!

He finally tried to sleep. The animals were resting well, so maybe there was nothing to it after all. At least, he tried to fool himself into believing such was the case.

Shortly after midnight, he awakened from a shallow sleep and felt an urge to walk a short distance from the camp. As he gazed out at the full moon and in the direction where most of tomorrow's work was to take place, he saw a ghostly haze creeping up from the creek bottoms over the whole of the area.

The eerie scene made him all the more concerned. He tried once more to get some rest, but was up again well before dawn. Off in the distance, a rooster was crowing and the full moon was setting on the far horizon. The morning sun was still hidden with only a predawn red glow slightly visible, but Big George was stirring. He was lighting the campfire while the others still slept. The cook would arise shortly and begin to prepare a hearty breakfast. It was hard work and the men needed all the calories they could get.

Soon O'Donnell arose and the remainder of the men left their knapsacks, strapped on their overalls and donned their shoes, wiped the remaining sleep from their eyes, and stirred about in an orderly fashion. Each had a set of tasks well-conditioned to him.

After the meal was consumed and the horses and mules were harnessed for the day's work, they all fell in line behind Big George.

"Gee hah" and all the other sounds made by the crews to the animals as they worked were sounds to behold - if you had never heard horse and mule teams work before. Occasionally, Big George would strike up a lead song and the others would join in. It helped to take away the monotony of the routine.

♦

The warm summer sun directly overhead signaled high noon and the workers were ready for a break and some food for their stomachs. They unhitched the animals, gave them water, and went to grab some midday chow. It was the usual dried pork with beans and rice, but it was edible.

Soon after the meal, the crews were at work again. The vines and brush had been cleared and by early afternoon, Big George was making his first cut in the red clay of an area north of the main dig. It would be used to fill an area back to the west to bring up the grade. The meandering Twelve Mile Creek had washed out many low places before it emptied into the Catawba River on its westward flow.

All was going well. It was taking time as it usually did. About two hours later and about four feet down, Big George's pan hit something solid. As he gazed down to take a closer look, his knees weakened and he felt his body flush. He pulled hard on his mules and hollered for them to stop, but before they did, he struck the second object. He looked down again. There before him were two skulls... seeming to stare directly at him.

Were they digging in a graveyard!? Was it an old Indian burial ground!? They had not been told to look out for any such thing.

Was this the fulfillment of the omen he had the night before!? Had the resident ghosts talked to him!?

Big George backed his mules up and moved them off to the side and he told the others behind him to do the same. He wasn't about to further disturb the dead.

"Goes and git de boss man!!" Big George yells out to one of the other workers, "and hurries up!" For once in his life, he was badly shaken – almost beyond his ability to maintain a bit of calm within himself, but he did. Big George leaned on his mule and wiped the sweat from his face. It was not the heat of the day causing the sweat which now flowed freely from his brow.

Soon, O'Donnell reached the site and was pulled aside by Big George.

"Boss man, we done scraped up a graveyard!!" George said in an apologetic but excited voice. "Come over heres and look!!"

O'Donnell, Big George, and the curious crew looked on to see what had upset George so badly. O'Donnell paused for a moment and told his crew to take the horses for a drink of water from the makeshift drinking trough. He also told one of the men to get him a shovel so he might take a closer look at what had been uncovered.

Carefully, O'Donnell dug around the bones to search for clues as to what they have dug into. They completely uncovered the two bodies belonging to the skulls. What he saw was strange... and disturbing.

"Boss man, there is evil here. Ise feels it with all my bones!!" George states emphatically to O'Donnell. "It jus ain't right! I ain't never seen fokes buried without no box and no clothes and dem two skulls both looked like they'd been hit in the same place wif a hammer!! No, it jus ain't right!" Big George shakes his head and walks a few steps away.

The foreman is not quite sure what to do. If they had dug into a Native American burial ground, the Native Americans would be upset. If they had dug into a church burial ground, the folks nearby who might have relatives there would be upset. For the time being, they would cover up what was exposed and try to find someone local to ask just who had been buried there.

O'Donnell gives a new set of work instructions to Big George and the workers, mounts his horse, and slowly rides away not knowing exactly what to do or where to start to do it.

CHAPTER THREE

The Curious Strangers
1887-1888

O'Donnell isn't sure what he needs do. He knows he must do something. He wonders where he might find someone who would be familiar with the area and could possibly tell him if his crew has dug into a forgotten burial ground. He notices the remnants of a partly overgrown old dirt road and decides to follow it. Shortly after he starts, O'Donnell meets a neatly dressed older Black man who appears out of a growth of bushes.

Startled, he stops and decides to quiz the man, "Might there be anyone around I could talk to about a situation on the property where we're digging?"

O'Donnell is astonished when the stranger blurts out a question of his own. "You found 'dem bones, didn't ya mista?"

Still shocked, O'Donnell, not wanting to give anything away, responds coyly, "And what bones might ye be talking about?"

The stranger replies, "Mr. Milton's graveyard!"

"And who is this Mr. Milton?" O'Donnell's curiosity is whetted now many times more than before because someone knows something about the burial site.

"Mr. Milton Chaney - who done kilt all dem folks and nobody didn't try to do nothin' bout it!" the stranger said in a convincing voice.

Big George's words suddenly rang strongly in O'Donnell's mind. *"They looked like they'd been hit wif a hammer. Somethin' evil here!"*

"How might ye know all this?" O'Donnell further quizzed the stranger in a sharper voice.

"I been watchin' you diggin'," came the reply.

O'Donnell was now all the more curious. He asked, "Who is this man named Milton Chaney?"

The stranger replied emphatically, "Mistah, I thinks I done told you too much already. I thinks I better hush. I told you what I telled ya 'cause I suspects you ain't from around here and you don't mean me no harm."

"Well, might ye tell me about anyone who can tell me more about *the bones* and Mr. Milton Chaney?" O'Donnell quizzed the stranger again.

"Mistah, if you follow dis road for about a haff mile or more, ther will be a big white house. The man der can tell you all you ever wants to know... but mistah, he ain't gonna tell you nothing... and mistah, you might not ought to ask him nothing neither," came the puzzling reply.

O'Donnell was becoming more confused by the moment. He wasn't quite sure how much credibility to put in what he was being told, but at the same time, this man spoke as though he knew what had happened. *Why would this stranger not tell him more? Why was he being directed to a house where a man knew all O'Donnell needed to know, but the man there wasn't going to tell him anything?*

"And mistah, please don't tells him you talked wif me. I don't thinks he can harm me much now, but I don'ts want to take no chances. No sirah, I don'ts want to take no chances at all," came the last statement as the stranger began to walk away.

"Who might you be?!" O'Donnell shouted – attempting to get in one last question.

Without an answer, a baffled O'Donnell parted and rode off down the old road. He looked back, but the stranger was gone. As quickly as the stranger had appeared, he had disappeared.

Soon, O'Donnell did, in fact, see a large white house a distance away. It was surrounded by mostly untended fields which looked as though, in the past, they might have yielded good cotton crops or whatever would have been profitably grown.

As he got closer and closer, the once grandiose house appeared run-down and ill-kept. O'Donnell wondered if anyone lived there at all. The front door was in disrepair and many of the windows were boarded where glass had once been.

He dismounted, tied his horse, and walked up on the porch, carefully avoiding what appeared to be weakened boards which might never support his weight. He knocked on the door and waited. There was no response from within. He knocked once again and still no one answered. Just as he was about to walk away, he heard the floor creak and the front door rattle and open. He turned to see a raggedy old man with an eye patch, stooped and bent, squinting to see who had knocked.

"What ye after?" the man asked in a sharply gruff voice.

O'Donnell turned and went closer to speak. "I was wondering if you might know," O'Donnell abruptly changed the intended question, "how far the creek just west of here goes north?"

"Mistah, hits been so long since I been about the creek, I can't remember," came the sharp reply. "Now if'n it's all ya wanna know, I'll be biddin you good day!"

O'Donnell, on the spur of the moment, had thought it best not to mention what he had originally come to ask. His gut told him it was the wrong person from whom to seek answers. Maybe the initial greeting had factored into his decision as well. He felt he should have taken the stranger on the road at his word.

He carefully walked from the porch, mounted his horse, and began his journey to the work site. On his way back, he looked intently for the Black stranger, but there was no sign of him.

He wondered why a man had volunteered information, especially if he felt he still might be in danger. Curiosity dictated another talk to the stranger on the road, if he could find him. O'Donnell looked for a place where the man might live, but he didn't see one. He became all the more puzzled.

When O'Donnell reached the work site, Big George had recomposed himself and the men were leveling out a different area well enough for the final grade. The two men talked and decided the less said about the incident, the better all would be. But neither could let it go so easily.

There was still the question of what to do with the remains. They were clearly on the right-of-way. They would have to be moved. O'Donnell would need to talk to his bosses to see what to do with the bones, unless he could determine a suitable remedy to the problem himself.

He and Big George were men of faith and each felt an obligation to see to it the bones were given proper attention and respect.

They found a secluded area away from the other men and began to talk

"Big man, strangest thing happened when I rode off just a while ago. I met a Black man on the road who had been watching us dig and he seemed to know an awful lot about the remains we'd found. He said they was in a Mr. Milt's graveyard. Seemed to think a man had killed these people," O'Donnell confided in Big George.

"Boss man, I telled you they is evil here! Them peoples looked like they been kilt and place there! I just got this strange feelin'. Boss man, what's we gonna do with dem bones!?" Big George asked.

"Big man, I'm not sure, but we gotta do something. I guess we need to go to the county sheriff. Strange thing though, big man, the stranger said nobody had tried to do anything about it. Still wonder what he really knows. Seemed scared somebody might know about him. Don't reckon he had anything to do with it, do you?" O'Donnell asked.

"Boss man, I don't rightly know. Mighta been fraid peoples gonna blame him for sumpin he didn't do. Black fokes gotta be careful. They still gotta fears for they lives at times," Big George replied.

◆

Perhaps a good night's rest would clear their minds of the shock and frustration finding the bones had brought. They could decide a course of action in the morning – yes, that was the best thing to do under the circumstances.

CHAPTER FOUR

O'Donnell and Big George
Meet Sheriff Haile the Third
1887-1888

Thaddeus O'Donnell finally decided the only proper thing to do was to visit the sheriff of Lancaster County. It was in his territory. The sheriff should be able to tell O'Donnell what he needed to do about the bodies. It was an all day trip to and from the county seat in the city of Lancaster 17 miles to the south of the railroad site.

♦

The horses were saddled a little after daybreak. Thaddeus O'Donnell and Big George grabbed a bite of breakfast and were soon on their way southward. They could be back within a day's time, if all went well.

"Aye, it looks to be a purty day for riding, wouldn't ye say, big man?" O'Donnell quizzed Big George.

"Shore nuff does, cap'n," came the reply from Big George, "but I fears we might still gets a storm later today, boss man."

"We can deal with a storm, big man. We have dealt with them before," Thaddeus O'Donnell reassured Big George. He was thinking too much about other things to worry about the weather, but he would keep the possibility of one in his mind since Big George had thought it important enough to mention.

♦

The ride was uneventful, although it was still long and tiring. The road was up and down hills and there were a couple of creeks to cross, but the courthouse was not hard to find. Such a grand courthouse it was. It had been designed by a premiere architect of the time, Robert Mills, who also had a claim to fame for designing the Washington Monument and other buildings in Washington, DC. Most people who visited the courthouse didn't pay much attention to who had designed it; they were usually there for other reasons – mostly run-ins with the law.

When they reached their destination, Thaddeus O'Donnell and Big George tied their horses to the first hitching rails they could find and started up the many steps to the front entrance.

"And where might we find the good sheriff?" O'Donnell asked the first person he saw whom he felt might give him a good answer.

"He'd be yonder at the jail," said the stranger as he pointed in the direction of a building with an open area next to it.

The jail had also been designed by Robert Mills, but it was not quite as elegant as the courthouse. Maybe the hanging area near it took away from its charm.

O'Donnell and Big George made their way to the jail just as a man with a badge was coming out the door.

"Pardon me, sir, but might you know where I could find the sheriff?" O'Donnell asked.

"And who might be looking for him?" came the reply from the man.

"My name is O'Donnell, and I'm looking for him on an important matter."

"Well ya found him. Haile's the name. And jus' what might be so important it would keep me from going to the courthouse to see about a prisoner on trial?" The sheriff said in a sharp tone.

"Might we talk in private?" O'Donnell suggested.

"It'll need to be quick, mista. Like I said, I need to get to the courthouse. Step over here," the sheriff said as he motioned toward an isolated area. "Is it about the Negro?"

"No, sir, it's not, and he can hear all we gotta talk about. It's about bodies in a graveyard," O'Donnell responded.

"Mistah, what bodies in what graveyard are ya talkin' about?" the sheriff quizzed sharply again.

"Up north from here, up where we're building the railroad," O'Donnell responded politely.

The sheriff raised his brows and looked directly at O'Donnell. He became considerably more interested. He knew where the railroad was being built. His deputies and travelers coming through town had kept the people in the city informed about the progress.

"Exactly... where are you talking about?" the sheriff asked in a more reserved tone now.

"Alongside an old shack near where the old north-south road used to be up in the Osceola region. We was wondering if we might have dug into an old church graveyard or an Indian burial site. The railroad don't want the publicity if it was to get out we had destroyed a graveyard," O'Donnell said apologetically.

The sheriff perked up more noticeably, twisted the end of his mustache, moved his hat slightly back on his head, and looked straight into O'Donnell's eyes, all the while thinking: *"Could this possibly be the bodies of the missing people who were rumored to have disappeared which he had heard his grandfather talk about when he had been sheriff and his father talk about when he was sheriff?"* Maybe it wasn't folklore after all.

Anxiously, the sheriff stated, "Mistah, maybe I'll be riding up your way first thing tomorrow morning. I'll expect you to show me all of what you talking about. Tell you what let's do in the meantime. Let's you, me, and the Negro go git some chow. If you hungry, there's a place near the edge of town we might go fetch good eats. They'll even let the Negro eat out back near the woods. We might sit there and talk a spell. I'd be mighty interested in what else you got to say."

To this courteous offer, O'Donnell replied, "I'd be mighty grateful to ye." He didn't know just how much of an intense interest he had sparked in the sheriff.

◆

They were soon off to an older building a short distance from the jail. It looked as though there had once been a much more grandiose establishment there. If fact, one of the grandest inns anywhere about had once been there. It had been advertised in all the papers within 50 miles of the site. However, its heyday was long gone and it had fallen in disrepair during the War Between the States. What could be salvaged was. For sure, the folks who now occupied it knew how to cook, and the folks around showed their appreciation by being good patrons.

Once they had dismounted and tied their horses, the sheriff again anxiously started to question O'Donnell.

"Mistah," the sheriff began, "where exactly agin did you say you found the bodies and how many of them do you think there might be?" The sheriff was double checking to be sure he had not jumped the gun. Maybe he was reassessing to be sure it wasn't too good to be true.

"Like I said, they were not too far from an old shack off in a patch of vines near a growth of small cedar trees and bushes," O'Donnell replied. "I don't know just how many there might be. It looked to me as though there could be more than what we uncovered."

"Guess I really do need to ride up there tomorrow," the sheriff responded.

♦

During the meal, the sheriff bombarded O'Donnell with more questions, a few of which seemed odd. The questions also indicated the sheriff just might know more than he was telling. *Was the sheriff's promise to take care of the matter so quickly somewhat unusual, or was he just eager to do his job?*

The sheriff finally did make a formal introduction to O'Donnell. His full name was Baron Haile the Third. He had been named after his father and his grandfather. All the people around had called him Barry since he was a youngster. Realizing O'Donnell was obviously Irish, the sheriff was quick to point out he was a descendent of the Scottish Haile ancestry and not the English. The sheriff's elaboration sparked a laugh from both.

The sheriff must have forgotten about the trial. He seemed much more interested about the bodies than O'Donnell had imagined he might be, especially after what the stranger on the road had said.

O'Donnell, too, was beginning to rehash the thought of the stranger: "You done found Mista Milton's graveyard, ain't you?" Maybe there was more to it after all. Why had the stranger said nobody wanted to do anything about it? It all seemed more than a little odd at the moment.

O'Donnell still didn't tell the sheriff about his encounter with the stranger. Tomorrow, the sheriff would be where they were working. He wanted to get all of this straight in his mind before he let go of any more information. The unusual interest by the sheriff had caught him off guard. Yes, tomorrow would be a better time to say more, if anything at all.

♦

The meal was finished, kind words were exchanged, and O'Donnell and Big George both thanked the sheriff for the hospitality. They rode back toward the court house. Just before they parted on their separate ways, the sheriff thanked O'Donnell once again for telling him about the bodies.

The afternoon had gotten hot again. Just as Big George had said there might be, there were storms off in the distance as they rode up and down the hills back toward the campsite.

"Big man, are ye certain the bodies we saw had been hit with a hammer?" O'Donnell quizzed Big George again.

"Boss man, I tells ya, what we saw was evil. I feels it in my bones. I done seed the look on dat sheriff's face when you told him about where dem bones was. There's more to it than just bones!" Big George expressed in an uneasy voice.

If there was any certainty to any of this, it was the fact O'Donnell knew Big George had never, not even once, been wrong in whatever he had told him.

O'Donnell's mind now became fertile ground for all sorts of thoughts about where this might lead. Still, he had to dispose of it as quickly as possible. He was getting paid to build a railroad, and the big bosses wanted it all done as quickly as possible.

He could justify what he had done thus far. The bodies were on the right of way and they needed to be moved. Removing them and getting them to another place with an honorable burial would be the proper thing to do. O'Donnell would settle for nothing less.

What else was going on in O'Donnell's mind? Was he satisfied he and Big George had completed their obligation? Could he be completely satisfied until... ?

CHAPTER FIVE

The Sheriff's First Visit
1887-1888

Early the next day, the railroad crew was up and working. There would be no more digging in the immediate vicinity of the old inn until the situation with the bodies was squared away. Big George was in the lead, they were in full rhythm, and it was as though nothing unusual at all had happened two days before. O'Donnell was checking the grade to be sure it was within tolerance and thinking of how the next miles might be better negotiated to make best use of the labor. He had an outstanding relationship with the men. He expected a day's work and he rewarded them with proper pay, food, and respect for their labor.

About eleven o'clock, O'Donnell was startled as he saw a group of men on horses along with two wagons approaching the campsite. Soon, he was able to clearly see it was Sheriff Haile. The others were unknown.

"Good day to ye, gentlemen," O'Donnell greeted them in a pleasant tone. "I'm suspecting you're here about what we talked about yesterday."

The sheriff nodded and said, "You'd be right, sir."

"I see yer horses are a bit winded. Thar's good water in the spring yonder alongside the road. Ye might take yer horses there and refresh yourselfs as well," O'Donnell suggested.

O'Donnell pointed the way and the men were quick to take him up on his offer.

After the animals were cared for, there was more small talk to start the serious dialogue both knew was forthcoming.

"Let's go yonder just toward the old shack," O'Donnell stated as he pointed in the direction of the old inn.

The men started walking and were soon at the site where the first graves had been uncovered. Sheriff Haile was almost certain - if there were bodies near the old tavern, they were not in a legitimate burial site for a church, Black or White, and they certainly were not in an Indian burial ground. They had to be something out of the ordinary.

"So there really were bodies and this is where he hid 'em," the sheriff muttered and shook his head as though he was highly disgusted because no one had ever found the graves. He was indeed surprised there really were bodies. *So... all the talk of Milt Chaney's involvement with the missing people was not just rumors started by the locals.*

"My granddaddy was right," he thought out loud.

But then again, it was not quite as simple as he was thinking. It was a complicated story to be sure, and to be truthful, no one had ever had any real reason to look in any particular spot and no one had ever pressured the authorities to look so close to the inn. There were other stories, too. Many of which were started by Milt Chaney and people nearby – "there were highway robbers operating out of Kershaw (to the south) and Waxhaw (to the north) who accounted for the disappearances."

Most people around felt if there had been bodies to be disposed of, they probably were taken off deep into the woods for the creatures to ravage. Others felt that most likely the bodies had been dumped in the Catawba River. There had been a few bodies seen floating down the river about the same time people had disappeared. *There was all sorts of speculation.*

The sheriff himself had heard different stories from his father and his grandfather. The present Sheriff Haile was the third generation to be elected to the office. Evidently, the people had been satisfied with the family's service.

During the tenure of his grandfather, the sheriff's main obligation had been to help with horse thieves, slave stealers, and run-away slaves. It was during his generation the crimes had occurred and Milt Chaney had been hanged, but oddly enough, not for killing anyone. Then again, the remoteness of the region during the time of the disappearances made the happenings there almost insignificant to the majority of the people who lived in the middle of the county near Lancaster.

When his father was elected in 1860, the talk of the possibility of war was in the forefront of every conversation and any mention of Milt Chaney and the likes was only in passing thought. Over the years, it had all been forgotten, except by a few folks in the area around where the alleged crimes were thought to have taken place. *Maybe some of them still had to be concerned about the possibility they might eventually see justice at the end of a rope.*

But, as time passed, if there were guilty others, they must have felt they had escaped judgement – well, at least earthly judgement.

Had it not been a family matter and the youngest Sheriff Haile looking at this as though it might have been a failing on the part of his grandfather, he might not have been so interested. He had loved his grandfather and had heard one or two folks belittle his grandfather and his father about the fact neither had solved murders and the strange disappearances of the travelers; therefore, neither deserved reelection. Was the present Sheriff Haile's real concern the vindication of his grandfather and his father?

"How many bodies do you think there are?" the sheriff again quizzed O'Donnell.

"I'd have no real idea. Like I said before, we only dug up two before my man George became upset and felt we needed to contact the local authority about 'em. We both looked close enough to realize the two people seemed like somebody had knocked a hole in their heads. Strangely too, we didn't see any signs they had been buried in a box or with clothes," O'Donnell stated.

"You did the right thing. You did what you was supposed to," the sheriff repeated as he twirled his mustache. He was glad for more reasons than he ought to be.

"Boys, let's get the shovels and picks to see if there are others," the sheriff told his men. "If there is, we'll need to get more men and wagons up here to do what's right by the remains. The railroad'll be wantin' to use this land."

It was at this time O'Donnell realized he was caught up in a situation and he wanted to know the details of what it was all about. He could stand it no longer and he pulled the sheriff aside and began, "Sir, might ye tell me what really went on here? I'm a lot curious and puzzled."

"Mistah, it's a long story and you got every right to know. When we get time, we gonna sit a spell and I'll tell you all I can. I ain't sure of it all myself, but I'll share what I do know," the sheriff promised O'Donnell.

The sheriff felt he owed O'Donnell an explanation. After all, finding the bodies was a colossal occurrence.

O'Donnell now became even more curious. Was Big George right about *some kind of evil* being responsible for the bodies buried there? He wanted to find out as much as he possibly could.

"When do you suppose we might have our conversation?" O'Donnell asked rather pointedly.

"Well, I tell you, when we find out how many people are buried here and we get them all moved to a decent burial place, we'll talk. We gonna need a long time, mistah, We'll need a while," the sheriff said as he shook his head.

O'Donnell gave the sheriff a strange look, nodded, and walked away. He looked back from a distance and watched the men continue to dig. They dug late into the afternoon. He could wait. He felt sure the sheriff would tell him later.

O'Donnell eventually mounted his horse and rode down the line toward Waxhaw. He needed to find a suitable place to bed three or four of the men for the night and maybe look for a future campsite.

CHAPTER SIX

But Who Were They?
1887-1888

The final tally was twelve poor unfortunate souls. Bedeviling questions remained: *Who were they? What had actually happened to these unfortunate people? Why had the evil man chosen these particular victims? Were there other unknown victims whose bodies had been left in other places? The unknowns were many!*

The sheriff and his crew had recovered the last of the remains and returned to Lancaster. O'Donnell could once again give his full attention to constructing the railroad.

Any place which looked as though it might hide remains and some places which didn't look suspicious at all had been turned with a shovel. The sheriff wanted to remove any chance of leaving a body or anything which might provide a clue about what had taken place at this dreadful venue.

No doubt, finding the bodies had created more questions which could never be answered. *Would it have been better just to let them rest or was finding the bodies predestined so the spirits might finally be freed?*

Why had the sheriff not explained everything he did know about the situation to O'Donnell and Big George? Questions abounded and there were no answers, at least none for O'Donnell.

◆

It had been a week or more since the sheriff had

taken away the last remains. He did at least tell O'Donnell he would "find them a fittin' restin' place." Maybe they were taken somewhere decent. Maybe they were taken to be looked at. Who knew?

The railroad crew had moved steadily. They had found a new campsite and all seemed to be going well. O'Donnell, Big George, and the crew had put any thoughts about the episode near Osceola in the back of their minds - until they looked up one afternoon and saw the sheriff, a deputy, and a man who clearly looked as though he was not a lawman.

"Good day to ye," O'Donnell said as the men approached. "I trust ye had a good ride up. If yer needin' water for yer horses, then there's some over in the trough."

"We stopped at the creek just back a ways," the sheriff replied.

"What brings ye back up here?" O'Donnell asked, even though he felt they were there to ask more questions and just maybe tell him whatever they might want to about the bodies.

"Mistah, I made you a promise a while back. I said I'd be telling you what we'd done with the bodies and what we think mighta gone on with the killing of them people. Well, I'm here to tell you. Might you have time late today or tonight?" the sheriff asked.

O'Donnell was exceptionally curious as to what the sheriff had done with the remains and what else he might tell him about the killings. He would make time to listen, so he told the sheriff, "I'd be mighty interested in whatever ye might have to say. Thar's shade over thar near the rocks. We'll be eating chow not too long from now and ye look like you'd be hungry."

"And you'd be right, sir," the sheriff responded.

Sheriff Haile introduced the deputy and there was a new twist. "I'd like ya to meet Reese Murphy. He's a newspaper writer with **The Lancaster and Camden Ledger.**"

Reese wore an old dress coat and his pants were a bit baggy. By his appearance alone, it would have been impossible to determine he was an excellent writer and knew how to shape a story for maximum interest.

Indeed, this was a new twist. *"Just what was a newspaper man doing here?"* O'Donnell thought to himself.

"Just in case you got the time to hear the whole story, or at least what we know, we brought our knap sacks and planned to stay the night. Would be mighty obliged if ya'd let us camp nearby. I know ya got work to do this afternoon, so I thought we'd talk round about the campfire tonight," Sheriff Haile said.

"I'd be glad to have ye and share what we got," O'Donnell was quick to answer. The boring everyday task of building railroad beds just became a lot more interesting. O'Donnell really wanted to know what they had started.

"Then I guess I'll be hearing a lot more tonight," O'Donnell said with grin.

"Mistah, you got a lot more to hear and this newspaper man wants to ask you and your Negro a lot of questions, too," the sheriff responded.

"Fair enough," O'Donnell said, "Ye take your time to find a place to tie yer horses for the night and put ye knapsacks while I check down the line a short ways. I ought not be gone too long."

While the workers went about their normal routine, the sheriff, his deputy, and the newspaper reporter looked for a suitable place to camp. They needed to take the saddles off the horses and feed them grain. They would need a campfire for themselves. O'Donnell and Big George would join them after the evening meal.

The visitors grabbed some coffee while the cook readied the chow.

◆

The last remnants of the evening shadows had given way to the night time. The moon crept up over the eastern sky and seemed to occupy the entire horizon. The cloudless night let the entire brightness of the full moon illuminate the area. *Fate had produced a perfect setting for the campfire stories.*

CHAPTER SEVEN

The Long Fireside Talk
1887-1888

The shadows cast from the light of the campfire and the full moon made the night seem all the more spooky. The meal was finished. The workers went about their last chores, readying themselves to turn in for the night and O'Donnell and Big George made their way to the sheriff's campfire.

The sheriff, his deputy, and the newspaper man had found a comfortable place to lean against - makeshift back braces. What would prove to be a long interesting tale was about to begin.

"Well, mistahs, get as comfortable as you can," the sheriff started. "You are about to hear things you won't believe. Would you think all them bodies you and us found was murdered by the man who ran the tavern?"

"My granddaddy was sheriff when it all took place more than thirty years ago. He was thinking all the time them people who was disappearing in these parts was being robbed and killed when they stayed the night at Chaney's place. He never could get enough proof to charge the man and put him on trial," the sheriff said.

"Fokes in these parts never would tell my granddaddy much of nuthin'. Most of the ones who might help felt my granddaddy's only job was to get their Negros back if they run away," Sheriff Haile said in a mildly disgusted tone.

O'Donnell grabbed another piece of wood and put it on the fire and the embers sparked into the air. The October night had a slight chill to it, and the fire felt good. He turned to the sheriff and stated, "Well, I suppose the times were a little different back then than they are now," as he sat back down to listen to what else the sheriff had to say.

"Well, if it had not been for Negro stealing, Ol' Chaney might never have been stopped from killing. I guess it's the main story I can tell you... 'cause my granddaddy helped hang him for it," Sheriff Haile said proudly.

"You won't believe how it all happened. It might not have happened at all if'n he hadn't stole a young buck named Toney and sold him off to a man in Virginia," the sheriff continued.

"It seems the young buck was supposin' to marry a real good lookin'- and I mean real good lookin'- young slave girl named Chloe Jane - and after he was stole and sneaked off to Virginia, he somehow convinced the slave master and the sheriff up thar that he'd been stole," Sheriff Haile said as he looked at the others.

"Before the sheriff had time to check anything out, the Negro Toney escaped and came back down here to his rightful owner. Everything still might have been all right, but the slave master there found out where this young buck had come back to and it went from there," Sheriff Haile continued. "The slave master sent his sheriff down here to collect the money for the slave. Chaney didn't have it. The sheriff from up there and his man rode on to Lancaster and told my granddaddy about the Negro stealer."

"It wasn't long before this got out and all the big men wanted Chaney hanged. They done figured out all along it was him who had been responsible for the stealing and selling more of their slaves. Now my granddaddy didn't know it was Chaney for shore, but he had to do what the big people wanted him to do or they mighta lynched Ol' Chaney themselves," Sheriff Haile said.

O'Donnell spoke up, "Sheriff, ye say it was all about one Negro named Toney. Would the Negro Toney be alive today?"

"A mighty fine question, mistah. After all the mess after the wah and all the Negros going here, there, and yonder, I can't rightfully tell you I'd know. It being such a long time ago, I just couldn't tell you," Sheriff Haile answered.

Had O'Donnell thought his strange coincidence of meeting the Black man on the road, especially since he had been *spying* on them digging, might have been connected somehow? If he did, at least for the moment, he didn't say anything.

"Sheriff, did this man Chaney have any help in stealing these slaves and maybe in all the killin?" O'Donnell questioned again.

"Another good question, mistah. Mor'n likely he had plenty of help, but he never admitted to any, so no one 'cept Chaney was hanged for it," Sheriff Haile responded.

"And the hanging, mistah, turned out to be somethin' talked about and wrote about for a while. Yes, sir, mistah, people gossiped about it for a long time. I speck some of the gossip added words to the truth." Sheriff Haile said with half a laugh as he shook his head.

"My granddaddy saved all the newspapers he could

with anything about Chaney in 'em. He put 'em in a safe place. I saw 'em one day when I was a youngin'; maybe it's what made me want to be a sheriff when I growed up," Sheriff Haile said with a reflective tone of voice.

"I tell you, mistah, people talked about the hanging for a while," Sheriff Haile continued. "They brought Ol' Chaney up on charges and he was guilty afor they ever finished the case. Wadn't nobody gonna put up with Negro stealing. The rich fokes was afraid if'n one got by wit it, then they'd lose all their slaves. Slaves meant money for the rich fokes."

"My granddaddy said he thought the man who testified agin Ol' Chaney was as guilty as Chaney, but since everybody thought if they got the ring leader, then the stealing would stop... and it did," Sheriff Haile continued with a raised concern in his voice. "Mistah, it was the first time in these parts fokes believed a Negro. But they believed Toney 'cause they wanted Ol' Chaney hanged."

"Well, Ol' Chaney did get himself a lawyer and they got the judges in Columbia to hear his appeal, but it wadn't too long before they all said he could be rightfully hanged and sent him back to Lancaster... and he was," the sheriff continued. "The old fokes who saw the hanging still talk about how crazy it was. Seems when he was asked if he had any last words, he ran his mouth for almost two hours. Fokes in the crowd hollered at him to tell about all the ones who had helped him, but he didn't say a word about nobody else, except when he finally read his poem."

"Mistah, I brung a copy of the poem wif me. If'n I can see by the light, I'll tell you what it said," Sheriff Haile said as he reached for his saddlebags.

"Hold on for a bit and I'll get a lantern so you can see," O'Donnell was quick to offer.

The sheriff pulls ruffled papers from his bag, positions them in the light of the lantern and starts: "Now this is what Ol' Chaney read right before they finally pulled the pin. They say the crowd got quiet as a mouse when he started. I guess everybody thought he might tell on somebody. Many fokes said maybe he did."

The sheriff clears his throat to put on his best voice and starts:

"My days are numbered they are but few
When I must bid this world adieu.
Dear wife, how happy I could be
If your dear face I could see..."
"On earth no longer I can stay
Because my life was sworn away.
His name, it's true, I can't conceal,
It was the one-eyed John Steele."

"I reckon you could say, Mistah, maybe he did name somebody who helped him, but there weren't no proof enough to do anything about it. Fokes just thought he's gittin' back at Steele for testifying agin him. But my granddaddy always thought Steele had helped him grab slaves and mighta done helped him kill people, too," Sheriff Haile continued.

"Sheriff, do ye think the man Steele might be alive?" O'Donnell quizzed.

"Well, mistah, funny you might ask, cause I heard fokes say he's still around these parts. My granddaddy always tried to check on him when he was in these parts, but like I said, the wah came and nobody thought about nothing but the wah for so long, he, like everything else, was forgot," Sheriff Haile said in a somewhat deflated tone.

"Did anyone keep a record of who any of the fokes were who disappeared?" O'Donnell quizzed again.

"Mistah, my granddaddy kept as many records as he could. He took em home wif him when he got wind the Yankees was coming through. I don't know if he got em all. The Yankees burnt part of the old jail, and what was lost, I can't rightfully say. What I can tell you is - there was fokes who came through Lancaster looking for their missing. I speck most of them fokes is gone themselves now. You gotta remember lots of them fokes was old back then and there was some whose fokes had no idea what to do and no money to do it with," Sheriff Haile offered his explanation.

"I can believe it," O'Donnell stated. "I understand. So I guess the story ends there."

"I'm supposin it does, mistah," Sheriff Haile followed up.

"I guess this newspaper man will write his story and it'll bring memries back to the old fokes and the young fokes can find out what happened in their own county and then it will all go away," Sheriff Haile finished.

◆

But would it? What had the sheriff and those before him not known?

◆

"Now, mistah, I done told you all I know about what went on. I speck Mr. Murphy might have questions he'd wanta ask you, if you don't mind."

"One last thing, sheriff, if you don't mind," O'Donnell asked, "What did you finally do with the bodies?"

CHAPTER EIGHT

The Paupers' Burial Grounds
The Late 1880s

Thaddeus O'Donnell was still considerably concerned about what the sheriff had done with the remains dug up at the old tavern. Maybe he felt responsible. After all, it was his crew who had disturbed them. When he questioned the sheriff about the final disposition of the remains, Sheriff Haile the Third was quite detailed in his answer to O'Donnell.

"Well, mistah, we finally put them in a graveyard outside of town. We had asked the fokes around Lancaster if they might help us find a good place and didn't nobody want to give them a fittin burial. Well, they wanted them to have a fittin burial, just not in their burial grounds. We took it on ourselfs to get what was left of each set of bones and place them in a separate box. Wad't no fancy box, but we had at least put each of them in a box," Sheriff Haile started.

"We had to finally place them out in our graveyard... the one used for people hanged when nobody came for the body, and for people who died and didn't have no kin to claim 'em and for people who didn't have no place to go," Sheriff Haile continued.

"We was careful enough to try to match the order of the bones in the way we dug 'em up. We put the bones in sacks. We put each sack in a box we got. We buried em' to match the order we dug 'em up. I think we done a pretty good job of it," the sheriff stated proudly.

"You know something, I don't know whether the old

graveyard had Chaney's bones in it or not. Might be a real strange thing if'n it does. Imagine if you can, a murderer havin' to sleep with them he murdered," the sheriff said with half a laugh.

"It would be a form of justice, I suppose," O'Donnell responded.

"But we don't know if it's the case," the sheriff replied. "Don't reckon we'll ever know any of them fokes what's been buried there. It's been such a long time and so many things has happened."

"Fokes say Yankees camped out there during the war. I don't know if'n they disturbed any of the graves. I think all the markers was gone when they got there," the sheriff rambled on. "Some fokes sneaked in and put up some kinda markers without a family name on it. They don't want nobody knowing who their kin was, I reckon. Felt some guilt not having nothing on the grave, I guess."

"Old fokes say the Yankees didn't attempt to stay there but one night. They got scared off by something during the night," the sheriff laughingly stated.

"I left a good-sized rock and a wooden marker at the head of each grave of the fokes we buried. Didn't know what else to do. Like I said before, nobody ever gonna know who they are anyway," the sheriff continued.

"Now, Mr. Newspaper Man," Sheriff Haile started as he looked at Reese Murphy, "you got to be careful just how you write this story. You can't say all of the things I been saying. You gonna have to polish everything up as best you can."

"Oh I'm not gonna make anybody look bad. You folks have been awful nice to me. I'm just gonna do my job and tell what I think is a good story about it," Reese

Murphy replied in his usual sincere and subtle voice.

"And I guess you'll need to be careful how you mention the railroad, too," O'Donnell was quick to inject.

"Gentlemen, I think everyone will be pleased with how the story turns out," Reese told them both.

◆

The cemetery was located in an area where people seldom traveled. Tall pines along with a few hardwoods and scrub trees surrounded the area. The graves which had been there for years were hardly recognizable. When the county chain gang had nothing better do, they cleaned up the area. The years of neglect and what little care it had gotten made it a shameful site.

Since the new graves had been put there, the sheriff had taken a special interest and was working with the prison guards to get inmates to work there more often. It was though he now felt he had an obligation to anyone who came looking for the bodies; it would not be a blight on his time as sheriff.

The names of all who were previously buried there were unknown. Time, along with circumstances, had forgotten them. Twelve more unknown souls, at least by those still living, had now been added to the list.

Were Milt Chaney's remains among those buried in the cemetery? There was a hush at the time about what had actually happened to his body after it was taken from the gallows. No one can remember if his wife and children claimed the remains or not.

Many of the records from the court house and the jail had been burned or went missing when the Union

Armies came through. The remaining records were sketchy at best.

Sheriff Haile had done his best to piece together what his grandfather and father had managed to save. He had also added, for better or worse, some of the things he had heard.

CHAPTER NINE

Milt Chaney and The Tavern
1849

Milt Chaney was, by the standards of any day, a huge man. His beard was long and always well-groomed as was his full head of reddish brown hair. It was characteristic of his Scottish ancestry. He was broad shouldered and as strong as the proverbial ox.

His survival and marketable talents were numerous. He could build and fix wagons, shod horses, and construct dwellings. To everyone's surprise who met him, he seemed to be an exceptionally intelligent and well-mannered man. He was a contradiction of sorts to anyone who tried to match his backwoods look to his well-developed language skills.

People in the area believed he had migrated to South Carolina from Virginia where his ancestors had arrived in the 1700s. He was thought to still have distant relatives who were tobacco farmers in the eastern part of Virginia. Why he had chosen this particular spot in South Carolina to settle was anyone's guess.

He had a wife from Monroe, North Carolina. She was 10 years his junior. She had grown up as a farmer's daughter and even though there was a rugged look about her, she could turn a man's head. They had built a small cabin in the woods back of where the tavern was eventually constructed. Records reflect three small children also lived there.

Milt Chaney had purchased this land in the upper part of Lancaster County with hopes of being a successful farmer and cashing in on his hard work. He had little, if any, money for labor and struggled while others near him enjoyed financial success in years when crops were plentiful.

There were sizable plantations throughout the area. The agreements with the Native Americans to farm the rich fertile land favored those who were politically connected. Milt Chaney was not one of them. It seemed as though he had gotten the worst pick of farmland. No doubt it was the reason he was able to buy it so cheaply.

Chaney had 50 acres with a portion of the land bordering 12 Mile Creek. The land bordering the creek was fertile, but it flooded unpredictably when the strong storms of summer brought heavy downpours. This would often ruin crops which had been laboriously planted and tended.

The other problem which eventually turned into a blessing, at least for Chaney, the *Great Road* as it was called, from Charlotte to Camden, cut through his property. George Washington had traveled this road with his stately coach and white horses into South Carolina. Colonial soldiers had used it during the Revolutionary War.

After three years of barely scratching enough from

the ground to feed his family, Chaney decided he had to do something different. He had almost reached a point where he was about to lose his land to the tax sales. If the land had been more productive, there is little doubt the greedy people around would have pushed the sheriff to serve papers on Milt.

Milt Chaney had seen the people moving along the road to their destinations north and south. He had seen them stop at the spring rock on the north slope of the hill at Osceola to get their fill of the cool spring water. He had watched as wagon drivers had camped on the public land near the creek.

He could provide services such as feed and other care for the animals of the travelers. He could even fix a wagon if need be. Maybe, just maybe, he might even offer a bed for the tired people. He could at least attract a certain type of traveler who didn't need a fancy place to spend the night.

Chaney was also good at another trade. He could make and serve his home-brewed alcohol. Most of the other inns nearby didn't serve the hard drink.

So the idea of *Milt Chaney's Tavern and Inn* was born. It proved to be a fateful decision in more ways than one and for more people than yet imagined.

♦

Milt Chaney got lumber from a local sawmill run by a man named Jim Wilson. The Wilson Sawmill didn't produce the planed lumber for the fine houses around. It was finished at another mill. The unfinished lumber was the only lumber Milt Chaney felt he could afford and even then, Milt would have to *work off part of the debt* until he got a cash flow.

Chaney put together a small building which was attractive enough for a particular type of traveler. Circumstances sometimes brought others who might have chosen to stay elsewhere.

When the rumor got out that the rough looking "shack" Milt Caney was working on was going to be a tavern to attract the weary travelers as they went to and from the towns and villages around, many laughed at such a ridiculous idea.

Such remarks as "Aint nobody gonna stop there when there's a fine place to stay jus' up the road 'bout three, three and a haf miles"... and "there's a mighty fine place in the Lancaster village wif a place to even park ya buggy out da weather" were typical.

Indeed, there were other inns on the stretch of road between Charlotte and Lancaster. In the village of Lancaster, the stop in 1832 was at Leroy Secrest's *Swan Tavern*. The *Camden and Lancaster Beacon* ran Secrest's ad promising "a House of Entertainment at the sign of the Swan." Swan Tavern was "large and roomy" with "a shed attached for carriages." Years later, Secrest filed a petition of bankruptcy in U. S. District Court. Apparently, his hopes to merit a share of public patronage didn't work out. There still were lesser inns in Lancaster proper which attracted travelers.

Sixteen miles up the road from Lancaster in the Belair community of Indian Land, David Hagins operated an inn. His inn was a first-class stagecoach stop. When a coach came within a mile of the inn, the driver would begin blowing his horn to announce the arrival. The horn was the signal for fresh horses to be harnessed and ready for the switch.

David Hagins' Inn prospered (it stayed in business until around 1900), but sometimes there were problems with the guests. Hagins, a devout member of Six Mile Presbyterian Church who never missed a service if he could help it, was away when four or five of the inn's guests began dancing on the broad piazza of the inn. The *sinful act* was reported to fellow church members and they were quick to tell the church leaders.

In spite of Hagins' protesting he had done nothing wrong and, indeed, was in church at the time and could not be held accountable "for the actions of passing strangers," he was summoned to appear before the officers to be disciplined. Tempers flared and Hagins quit Six Mile Church, never to attend again. In fact, he deeded six and a half acres off his Catawba Indian lease as a gift to the Reverend Adam Ivy and a group of Methodists who built a church now known as Belair United Methodist.

♦

No one ever determined just how well Milt Chaney was doing financially with his inn. He did get horses to lend, rent, or trade to the travelers who might have an animal go lame or develop a sore leg. He continued to do black smith work for travelers and locals in need.

The clientele who patronized his inn sometimes appeared to be a little questionable, but there was never trouble, even if they appeared to have consumed a little too much of Chaney's alcohol.

He gradually shifted more and more of his time away from attempts at farming toward the chores which the inn required to attract customers. Many of the customers would pay a return visit during the hauling and traveling season and some might even stay a third time there. Others were not quite so fortunate. *At times, a visit on a full moon was not a good idea.*

For the most part, his family usually stayed out of sight unless they were helping with the chores. Come sundown, they were safely tucked away in their small cabin in the woods and had no knowledge of what went on in the night time hours at the tavern.

CHAPTER TEN

The First Victim?
(1852)

"Alice, mah dear," John DeMars said to his lovely wife as he put away the magnificent gold timepiece she had so proudly given him for their tenth wedding anniversary, "I must be off to the office. I have an awfully busy day ahead."

John's gold watch had belonged to Mrs. Alice's father. She, the first born child of her family, loved the watch since her mother had first given it to Mrs. Alice's father many years before. It was passed on to Mrs. Alice after the death of her father.

It was an extraordinary timepiece from the finest watch makers in Europe. Interestingly enough, when her mother had it engraved, she had left a place large enough so there might be another engraving placed on the watch. Mrs. Alice had done so with: *To My Beloved John, forever, Alice.*

◆

John Mitchell DeMars had become one of the pre-eminent businessmen of the old Southern aristocracy by brokering the king of the crops, cotton. South Carolina was in the heyday of an era of plantation owners thriving in the latest luxuries of the times. Their profits were even higher when shrewd businessmen such as John got them top dollar in the markets.

John also realized there were profits to be made by working with the smaller farmers as well. He could get their production together and sell it at a competitive price to Northern mills and other buyers who needed the raw material.

He visited the fields and owners often to see what he might expect in terms of buying and selling the next crops. There were beginnings of other types of crops for rotation now, and he certainly was not going to miss an opportunity to be involved in anything with the possibility of a sizable profit.

♦

He had grown up in a more modest setting than had Mrs. Alice. John had worked himself into the gentlemen clubs because he had the business savvy to make money. His marriage into a prominent family and his financial abilities had gained him acceptance among even the most entrenched of the old Southern elite.

John DeMars caused many a lady to blush as he complimented those with whom he had just completed a dance at one of the balls or social gatherings. Many thought Mr. John, as he was often called, was a ladies man because of his flirtatious behavior. Most knew otherwise. He was a strong believer in the principles of his Christian up-bringing. He seldom partook of alcohol. Perhaps, if there was a special occasion, he would drink a small amount, but it was limited to a single glass – often unfinished.

He had moved to the society of Camden from the small city of St. Matthews, South Carolina. He had been exceptionally successful there, but he beckoned for something just a little finer. His wife Alice might have been happy to live out her days in St. Matthews and often told John she would be well-satisfied there.

Camden did have the ambiance of the fame which the Revolutionary War had brought. Descendants of famous battle leaders lived there as heirs to their glory.

Mrs. Alice fit in well and had the most lavish of home decorations. John had his rooms full of animal trophies he had gathered on his many hunting expeditions. He had renewed his interest in hunting when his grandson Carter reached an age appropriate for joining the elders on their jaunts.

John's two lovely daughters often accompanied him and Mrs. Alice on their travels near and far. He had established friends and business connections throughout the nation and world.

The young ladies had been able to attend the finest schools of the day. Christie, the younger daughter, had married her childhood sweetheart and they had a child whom they named John Carter. John DeMars had taken Carter under his wing after Carter's father passed away when the toddler was only five.

John spent time with Carter whenever his busy work schedule permitted. He taught him to ride, and when John felt the young man could safely handle a gun, he had a shotgun custom made for him.

◆

"Alice, mah dear, I have been in communication with my long term business acquaintance, Mr. Landrum Pigg from Charlotte, North Carolina. He will have business partners form Europe at his office this fall. He would

like for us to meet with him and their families if we can make arrangements to travel there, weather permitting," John DeMars said enthusiastically.

"We can also use part of the trip for a vacation of sorts and will have the pleasure of each other's company undisturbed. I thought you might like to come with me," John quipped with a smile.

"We shall see, but I definitely don't want to take a long trip in the coach if the weather will be a problem," Alice responded.

"Well, mah dear, we can arrange the trip after the summer storms and before the autumn chill sets in. I know you are not fond of the cold," John lovingly and lightheartedly said. "So I will plan on your company on the journey. It will make it considerably more enjoyable than having only James or Big Bart. They are good for manly conversations, but not much otherwise."

James and Big Bart were the family coachmen who had served for a considerable length of time. They were loyal and were compensated well for their services. John had given them papers as freedmen but wanted them to stay on. They were gathering age and certainly were not the strong horsemen they once were. There was little doubt, however, each could still be worthy of enduring a lengthy trip.

The actual trip was still months away and there was other business to attend to, such as making sure the home was ready for the fall storms and the winter weather. Usually the winters were mild, but there were times when the cold could be right harmful for those not prepared.

John's junior partner, Hayne Herndon, could run the business in John's absence. John had come to know

Hayne from a chance meeting in Elloree, South Carolina, while both were searching for horses at Gregory Smith's horse farm. Both knew the finest horses in the South were raised there. The farm had an excellent reputation over the entire east coast. They also trained fine race horses for the various enthusiasts from hundreds of miles around.

Hayne Herndon had his own transportation company. As he and John talked, both saw an opportunity for a business venture. The two businesses would complement the other and increase the wealth of both. So, with a gentleman's handshake, the partnership was formed. Hayne would do the hauling for John and John would find the markets for Hayne's existing customers.

◆

The couple of months had seemingly gone by rather quickly and the time had come to make the final preparations for the journey to Charlotte. Due to unforeseen commitments to a local women's social club, Mrs. Alice was not able to make the trip. John had decided since Mrs. Alice was not going, there was no need to take the big carriage; he could take the smaller one and only one coachman. The setup would be adequate for the journey. They could take their time and stop along the way.

What John thought to be adequate was always exceptional in quality. No doubt he had the finest horses which his friend Richard Smith had acquired and saved special for him. He had the carriage makers customize his carriage for durability and comfort. He had even been sure to have the best comfort for his coachman. Most people knew John's carriages and horses by sight.

♦

John said his farewells to Alice, and he and James, the older of the two coachmen, were on their way. Alice caught a final glimpse of the coach as it turned the corner headed for the last turn to the main road. Big Bart was left behind to do the chores and drive Mrs. Alice to places around town when she desired.

As was customary, John had taken his most trusted rifle and hand gun with him. James was armed as well. No one thought there might be any problem, but it never hurt to be protected in case there was a need.

The first leg of the trip into Lancaster was uneventful. There were hills to negotiate, but the road, for the most part, was well-kept because of the amount of travel.

The trip was planned in two legs. The first would be to the city of Lancaster and the second would be from Lancaster to Charlotte. Each leg was a little less than 40 miles. It would be a long day, but it could be handled if all went well and there were no unusual happenings.

♦

However, *fate* cast a different light on the second leg of the trip. About 15 miles north of Lancaster, one of the two horses appeared to be having trouble with one of its hind quarters.

"Mr. John, I thinks we need to stop and check out one of da hosses," James shouted into the coach.

"If you are concerned, then by all means we should," John shouted back to James. He knew James was one of the finest coachmen around and whatever he suggested should be done.

They found a wide enough place to pull the horses

and coach over. James climbed down from his perch and John exited the coach about the same time.

"Which one is it," John quizzed James.

"It's the gray one, Mr. John. I'll check his foot and leg all over, don't think it's nothing serious, but we needs to be careful on a long trip," James cautioned.

James looked the horse over thoroughly and said, "Mr. John, I think he can make it a couple more miles, but I'm shore he gonna need a night's rest. If'n we can find a place to camp for the night, we mights need to do so."

John DeMars had heard of an inn along the way near the Belair community. Maybe they might make it there and not need to camp for a night. If he had calculated right, it was three miles at the most. They could make it down the stretch to Osceola and the rest of the way might not be too bad. So, the plan was set. They would work it out, just as they always did.

◆

Unknown to John DeMars and most of the travelers was a new sort of shabby inn which had opened. It sat at the foot of the grade at Osceola Hill. It was run by a man named Milt Chaney.

◆

"Mr. John, I see'd a place up on the right side of the road. It look like they might be able to tell us how far we gots to go 'fore we find a place for the night," James called back to Mr. John as they neared the bottom of the hill.

As James pulled the coach closer to the rough looking dwelling, he could see a hastily painted sign over the front door which read *Chaneys Tavern & Inn.* At the same time he saw the sign, he thought to himself, "Mr. John ain't gonna want to stay at no place like this." However, they did need to stop.

John DeMars exited the coach, looked at James with a question on his face, and went to the entrance. Just as he was about to open the door, a huge man came round the corner of the building and, for a moment, John thought he might have a problem. Surprisingly, the man spoke in a mannerly tone.

"And what might I do for you mister? I'm Milt Chaney and I own this place. I know it looks a little rough, but we keep it clean and we offer mighty good service."

John DeMars didn't know quite what to say. The image he had first formed in his mind and what he had now heard from the man were in conflict. What was he to think? John had been on hunting trips and had stayed in far more rugged places and had seen men of all shapes and sizes, so he felt comfortable with this situation.

"I'm John DeMars," he responded. "This is my driver James. One of our horses seems to have a sore foot or leg... we might need to rest it for the night."

"Mistah, you'd be mighty welcome to spend the night here. I even got a place in the barn for your coachman. And if in the morning your horse is still hurting, I might lend you one of mine... if you'll be passing back through here sometime soon," Chaney continued. "Now let me take a look at your horse."

With those words, Milt Chaney approached the hurting animal, looked closely at the hind quarter, and told John, "Mistah, he's a mite swollen in the lower leg. You might oughta unhitch him and let him rest his leg awhile. Don't think it's anything real bad, but he don't need to travel no more today."

John looked at the leg again as Milt pointed out his concerns and agreed.

The more they talked, the more John DeMars was convinced this might not be such a bad place after all.

"Let me look at your stock in case I might need to take you up on your offer of a horse," John said to Milt.

"Round this way," Chaney replied, as he pointed to stables near the edge of the woods.

John walked over and looked at the horses. They were certainly not as fine as his, but there might be one he could use if necessary. There was feed for his horses there as well. It was at this time he decided he would spend the night.

He asked where James might bed down and Milt showed him a stable which was fairly accommodating. John was satisfied. They would stay here for the night, get an early start, and be in Charlotte by mid-day.

John looked around to the western sky, pulled the gold watch from his pocket to note the exact time. *Just as he did, a ray of the afternoon sun reflected from the case of the watch just perfectly to catch the attention of Milt Chaney. Milt cut his eyes toward John just in time to see him place the fine timepiece back in his watch pocket.*

"I'll be offering supper after a while for the two of ya unless you brought your own chow," Chaney told John and James. "You might find a comfortable place to sit for a while."

John didn't like to waste too much time. There was still a good deal of daylight left. This would give him an opportunity to look at the papers he had brought along with him. After all, it was a business trip.

John even began to look forward to supper. It wouldn't be an elegant setting, but he was certainly game to eat what was offered and knew James would go along as well, so he agreed to eat what Chaney might be serving.

◆

Supper was indeed not bad. They had surely eaten meals which didn't measure up to what they had just consumed. Each had their fill. James went away to bed down in the stables and Mr. John was shown his room for the night. He took one more glance at the eastern evening sky and noticed the soon-to-be-full moon creeping up on the horizon. He would need a good night's rest, rise early, and maybe get to Charlotte by mid-morning... if there wasn't any more trouble.

John DeMars felt comfortable with the decision he had made about spending the night at Milt Chaney's Tavern and Inn. The food had been pretty good as a matter of fact. He had survived far worse situations.

He dozed off for the night wondering what Milt Chaney might be cooking for the morning meal.

CHAPTER ELEVEN

The Search Begins
1852-1854

It had been more than a week and John DeMars had not returned to Camden and his lovely wife Alice. This was most unusual for a man of John DeMars' planning and punctuality. Not once on any of his trips had he not returned as he had planned, at least within a day's time. He had repeatedly told her, "Since you are not going, mah dear, I will definitely return within 5 days. I will make the trip as short as possible."

Mrs. Alice, as she had often done, took him at his word. She had no reason for doubt.

♦

Hayne Herndon, John's partner, knocked on the

door. "Mrs. Alice, I hate to bother you, but I was curious as to when Mr. John might be coming back?" Hayne was beginning to worry as well. He, too, had been told Mr. John would be returning within 5 days or so. It had now been 9.

"Hayne, do you think we might need to send people to look for him?" she asked with a worried look on her face.

"Mrs. Alice, I've been thinking the same thing for some time now. I have already taken the liberty of inquiring with an agency here in town. I'd like to go ahead and start searching, if you would concur," he stated.

Maybe Mrs. Alice would have already sent searchers to look for her husband, but she had entertained the foolish thought he might have extended his trip for a tryst with a young flirtatious lady named Amanda Hill who had left town about the same time as her husband John.

To the contrary, it was soon confirmed - Miss Hill had gone out of town to meet with her book publishing agent in Charleston. It seems she was far more comfortable with pen and paper than she was with a gentleman suitor. Valuable search time had been lost by not knowing this and suspecting she might have been anything more than a friendly casual acquaintance.

"Hayne, I think we need to start the search as soon as possible," Mrs. Alice firmly stated.

"Yes, ma'am, I'll see to it directly, and I'll send one of our best men with the investigator," Hayne said politely.

♦

Bright and early the next morning, two men searching for John Mitchell DeMars left Camden, South

Carolina, on their quest. They would leave no possibility unturned. Howard McTeer, who worked for John DeMars, would ride with Kenneth Hattaway, the owner of the finest investigative agency in Camden. Although he might have sent a another man who was excellent, Kenneth Hattaway took a personal interest in the case because he, Howard McTeer, and John DeMars had gone on hunting trips together. Kenneth and Howard were the best men to try to solve this mystery.

The two left Camden on a Tuesday morning, exactly 10 days after John DeMars had departed. They planned to take the same route they thought John would likely have taken. The trip might be lengthy because they planned to investigate any lead, however small. They had but one request of Mrs. Alice and her family - *please be patient.*

Kenneth Hattaway had a plan he felt would find John DeMars, if he was going to be found. They would actually start pretty close to Camden. There were rumors of unexpected wealth to some people in the settlement of Kershaw, which was just a few miles north of Camden. There may not be any connection at all, but Kenneth Hattaway needed to be sure the new found wealth was not from illicit gain - mainly John DeMars' property. John's coach, horses, and personal items would have been worth the proverbial *pretty penny.*

Kenneth had heard the names of people and decided he and Howard would pay a visit to the locale. He never really suspected John had gone missing so close to home. Surely there would have been the sighting of a horse or the carriage such as John's so close to home.

John DeMars was well-known far and about. Maybe the real focus should be in Charlotte. The big city was at least another day's ride away, and then again, maybe two days or more if they were to check out everything along the way.

After riding into an area near Kershaw, they came upon a horseman going in the same direction.

"Good day to you, sir," both Howard and Kenneth greeted.

"And how are you two gentlemen this fine day?" was the response from the stranger.

The horseman was surprisingly friendly and well-spoken, and the conversation started in earnest.

"How are the folks around these parts?" Howard asked in a probing manner.

"Folks around here are fine. They are honest, law abiding, and work hard for a living. Not too many have much, but nobody takes advantage of anyone. We do have some boys who found a little bit of gold up in the creeks around, but nothing to brag about. Folks thought they'd robbed somebody, but they are good people and wouldn't harm anyone. Sheriff checked it out and they had gotten their gold like they said," the stranger replied.

Kenneth looked at Howard and they both thought the man was honest.

Howard asked politely, "And what did you say your name is?"

"The name is Knight, David Knight. I was on my way to Lancaster to do business at the courthouse today. If you gentlemen are headed there, I can show you the shortest route."

"I am Howard McTeer and this distinguished

gentleman is Kenneth Hattaway," Howard offered.

Kenneth and Howard decided there was probably no reason to further investigate anything around Kershaw. Besides, this man might tell them as much as they needed to know. So the three pointed their horses in the direction of Lancaster and the decision proved to be fortuitous. David Knight provided a wealth of information which confirmed nothing of interest was to be found around the Kershaw area.

"Do you ride this trail and the main road to Lancaster much?" Kenneth asked.

"I ride it about three times a week," David answered.

"I'll bet you see many fine coaches and horses then, don't you?" Kenneth quizzed. It was a per chance question. Just maybe he had seen John DeMars.

"Mister, I see all sorts of people and animals traveling these roads. A man might see the finest to the worst on the main road," David replied.

"Well, did you ever see, say about 8 or more days ago, a fine carriage with two large horses, one grey and one white? It would have had a Negro coachman and one passenger in the coach," Howard quizzed.

"Strange you should ask, 'cause I did see something which looked exactly like what you are saying. Of course, then again like I said, there are lots of fine looking horses and carriages traveling along the main road," David remarked.

"Well, this was a fine carriage and pair of horses, and you would have remembered them if you had ever seen them," Kenneth replied. "Which way were they headed?" Kenneth knew he could at least narrow it down by the direction in which they were traveling.

"They were headed toward Lancaster; in fact, it might have been who you are asking about. Once they saw I was not up to any harm, they were fairly friendly for a while. I remember the man in the coach saying his name was John. I don't remember his last name. I had to part ways to go see a friend along the way or I might have rode with them all the way to Lancaster. Truth is, I was only with them for a short while," David said in a matter-of-fact tone.

Kenneth, with a wrinkle of concern showing on his forehead, asked, "You did say his name was John and you can't recall the last name. Are there any highwaymen on this stretch of road?"

"Yes sir, his first name was John and I'm sorry I can't remember the last name. As many times as I have ridden these parts, I have never seen or heard of anybody causing any travelers harm. And mister, I've ridden these parts many times," David Knight replied emphatically.

The ride continued until Lancaster was in sight and the three parted their ways. The two investigators thanked the man for the information and David Knight thanked them for the company during the ride. Kenneth and Howard were almost certain John DeMars had made it safely through the Kershaw area and there was nothing to worry about there.

In Lancaster, there were stately inns. More than likely, John had stayed at one. It would be a matter of checking to see which one. They were in luck. At the first inn they visited, it was confirmed a man named John DeMars had stayed there. The date of his visit was the day he left Camden. This would have been on his way north to Charlotte. After further inquiries, they felt sure he had not stayed there or at any of the other inns in Lancaster on his way *back* to Camden. It was now late afternoon and the two men decided they would rest in Lancaster for the night.

◆

Bright and early the next morning, they saddled freshly watered and fed horses which had been cared for by the stable hands at the inn and were on their way. The ride was steady and uneventful except for a few wagons they passed along the way.

When they went down Osceola Hill just before noon, they noticed two horsemen near the rock spring and stopped for a moment to get refreshed.

"How are you gentlemen today?" Howard inquired of two men just finishing drinking the cool spring water.

"Doing okay, mistah. What about yourselfs?" one responded

"Fine, thanks. Was wondering if you fellas ride these parts much?" Howard asked, hoping to get a helpful response.

"Been through here once or twice, not too often, though. Speck we had better get on our way. Hope you fellas have a good trip," the stranger said.

The conversation hadn't been the least bit fruitful, so Kenneth and Howard mounted their horses again and shortly were passing Milt Chaney's Tavern.

"Howard, you think John might have stopped there for any reason?" Kenneth asked light heartedly, thinking he would definitely not have stopped.

"I don't rightly know, wouldn't think so. Think we

oughta stop?" Howard responded.

"I don't see anyone about, maybe not," Kenneth replied to Howard.

Just after they had decided not to stop, a huge man appeared from around the corner of the building. They both pulled the reins and turned back without saying anything aloud.

They approached the man without dismounting. Maybe it would be only a short conversation, they thought.

"Pardon me, sir," Howard started, "do you run this establishment or might know who does?"

"I'm the owner and how might I help you?" Milt Chaney answered with anticipation of doing business with the two.

Howard continued, "We were wondering if you might have seen a nice coach come through this way about a week and a half ago. He had two fine horses anyone would remember... if they had seen them."

Howard knew the horses alone would catch most people's attention.

"I'm not sure if I know exactly what coach you might be talking about. There are many fine horses traveling this road," Milt Chaney replied.

Thinking John would probably not have stayed there for the night and since the man didn't seem to want to answer much after the initial greetings, the two bid Milt Chaney a good day and rode off. Kenneth was a little bothered and felt something wasn't quite right, but he put his mind at ease as they got farther away from the inn. Kenneth told Howard, "Maybe we just ought to go on to Charlotte straight away."

Milt Chaney had sensed early on the two men were

investigating the disappearance of someone and he wasn't about to give any information.

"If I remember correctly from what I was told, there is an inn in the Belair area about 2 to 3 miles farther north," Kenneth said to Howard, "Think we might ask there if we have time, but I'm thinking mostly we ought to look real hard around Charlotte."

In about 45 minutes time they had come upon the inn at Belair. When they arrived, they were still undecided as to whether or not they should stop. For whatever reason, they did.

When they first stepped onto the porch, Kenneth asked a man standing there, "Might you tell me who owns this establishment?"

The man replied, "I am the man you're looking for. David Hagins the name. And who might you gentlemen be?"

"Excuse my impoliteness, sir, I am Kenneth Hattaway and this is Howard McTeer.

Kenneth then asked, "Sir, could you tell me if a man in a fine coach with a Negro coachman and two stately horses might have stayed here about 8 or 9 days or so past?"

"Mistah, I pretty well remember everybody who stays here and I can't recall anyone fittin' the description you givin'," came the reply. "I did see a fine coach pass by about the day you mentioned. It was early in the morning. Like you said, it was a fine coach with a Negro coachman. It had a real fine white horse and a big red horse. Red horse wasn't quite the caliber of the white one, but it looked to be a pretty good animal. Mighta come from Waxhaw or there about. Hadn't seen 'em around these parts before. It was too early to be from Lancaster," David Hagins answered.

Howard and Kenneth thought for a moment, looked at one another, and for the time being, dismissed any thought of it being John DeMars. The red horse didn't fit.

"Thanks for your help, sir. I speck we need to be on our way if we're gonna make Charlotte before nightfall," Kenneth told the man.

"If you are in these parts again, we have good beds and food and can take care of the horses too," the innkeeper told the two men.

Kenneth and Howard acknowledged the offer and bid farewell with the tip of their hats and were on their way.

◆

What Kenneth and Howard had not realized at the time is: *they had stumbled across valuable information which neither of them could fit into the puzzle they were trying to solve.*

◆

It was near dusk and the lights of Charlotte made them realize they had reached civilization again. They needed to find a place to bed for the night and care for the horses. Tomorrow they would search for the whereabouts of a Landrum Pigg. John had made it clear that Mr. Pigg was one of the main business contacts he had wanted to see.

CHAPTER TWELVE

The Search Continues
1852-1854

Charlotte, North Carolina, in the 1850s was, among other things, noted as a textile town. Obviously, it was the main reason John DeMars had journeyed there. He had met Landrum Pigg on one of his many travels. Mr. Pigg was successful in own right and was about to enter into a contract for cotton which John would supply, or at least it was going to be the topic of their meeting. They both knew the railroads would soon make it possible for large shipments which meant a good deal more profit for both.

◆

The morning started out with the two searchers asking the manager of the inn where they might find the business establishment run by Mr. Pigg. The manager had informed them they should go to one of the mills in town called Concord Mill. Mr. Pigg had originally opened his first mill in Concord and subsequently named it Concord Mill.

"And what direction should we start to find this

mill?" Kenneth asked.

"Well, you might start by heading back out the main road for about half a mile and then look for wagons full of cotton which, more than likely, will be headed to one of the larger mills about this time o' day and the first one they will stop at is Concord Mill," the manager told them.

Kenneth and Howard thanked the man and they headed north. Just as the manager had said, they soon saw two wagons loaded with cotton in front of them. They followed the slow moving vehicles until they were pretty certain where they should be going and then rode off at a faster pace.

Shortly, they came upon a massive structure. The front entrance of the mill had a small office located behind a set of scales where the wagons were weighed before and after they unloaded their cotton. There was a large sign on the mill front indicating this was Concord Mill. It now became a simple matter of determining if Mr. Pigg happened to be there or an employee might be able to tell of his whereabouts.

The two men dismounted, tied their horses at a convenient hitching post, and went into the front office.

"Good morning, sir," Kenneth stated to an office worker who happened to look in his direction. "Might you tell us where we could find a Mr. Landrum Pigg?"

"Mr. Piggs' whereabouts is a good question, sir," came the reply. "Usually about this time of year, Mr. Pigg and his lovely wife are on a cruise to Europe. Might I be of help to you?"

"We need to talk to someone who might know if this mill or any of the other mills or a main office, if there is one, would know about a visit from a Mr. John DeMars from Camden?" Howard quizzed the man.

"Yes, sir, I could tell you about the visit. Mr. Pigg showed a Mr. DeMars around his mills here in town about a week or more ago," the clerk replied. "I think they were about to go into a business deal together. Are you gentlemen here to check on the cotton shipment? I think the contract they agreed to says we were supposed to get our first shipment from you in two weeks from the signing of the contract. We would be due cotton in 4 more days from now."

Kenneth looked at Howard as Howard was looking back at him. For the moment, neither knew exactly what to say next.

Howard spoke, "You say you have a contract with Mr. DeMars' name on it?"

The man answered, "I'm sure we do. I was looking at our shipments due list just yesterday and your contract is a rather sizable one. I'm not likely to forget it."

Howard looked at Kenneth and shook his head. "Not only do we not know where John is, but I now have to fill a contract for cotton and I don't know where John was going to get it."

Howard looked back at the man and asked, "Do you think we might see a copy of the contract or at least the details of how much cotton we are supposed to deliver?"

"I'd be more than glad to oblige, sir," the clerk responded. "Is there a problem, sir?"

While the man was busy transcribing the details of the contract, Kenneth   pulled Howard aside and told him they needed to get as much information from this man as they possibly could - especially information about when John left town, if it was possible.

As soon as the man had written the details, he presented the paper to the two along with a signed copy of a contract bearing John DeMars' signature. There was no doubt, John had been there and had signed the agreement.

"We hate to be a bother, but might you have any idea where Mr. DeMars would have stayed while he was here in town?" Kenneth asked the man.

"Well, sir, no doubt he would have stayed with Mr. Pigg and his wife in their cottage on the outskirts of town. Mr. Pigg usually has his guests stay there. It's a rather nice place, I hear," the clerk answered.

"He would have been safe there," Kenneth told Howard. "He wrapped up his visit here. Had to disappear after he left to return home."

Maybe this was all the good information they were going to get from the Charlotte area. The chances of people seeing him on the road in a bustling city such as Charlotte and remembering him were extraordinarily unlikely.

"Sir, you have been a great help. We will work on this contract and see the obligation is met," Howard said in an confident tone of voice.

"Just one more question. Do you have any idea what day it was when Mr. DeMars got here?" Kenneth asked.

"I'm not sure, sir. Mr Pigg had been expecting him one Tuesday evening, but Mr. Pigg was here alone on Wednesday. He came back by here on a Thursday and Mr. DeMars was with him then," the clerk replied.

Each of the two men looked at the other and thought maybe *they now had an important clue to work with.* Once again they bid the man good day.

♦

The two investigators found their way back to their horses, mounted them, and began to ride slowly off in the direction of home. Shortly, they stopped and had a conversation about what they needed to do and what information they had actually gathered.

"Well, we know John reached Charlotte," Kenneth said to Howard with a sigh. "We just don't know where he was last seen on the way home. We need to stop at every place we come across as we go back and ask again. It won't hurt to ask every stranger we see along the road either."

"I'll agree with you there partner," Howard replied. "We gonna make it to Lancaster on the way home before we stop, are we?"

"Not sure where we might end up before the night comes, not sure at all," Kenneth answered, sounding distraught.

Almost four hours into the journey, they were in the Belair community and decided to stop once again at the inn located there. Something the mill employee had previously stated had come back to Kenneth's mind. Maybe the fact John had been a day late, if the man was correct, and John had not had any other business, was of great importance. John had been emphatic about a five day trip. It would be four days of travel and one day of business. Such would not have been unusual for John. He was always to the point on his business trips. There was one other clue Kenneth was thinking about, perhaps it was paramount to the investigation.

Soon the inn at Belair was in sight and Kenneth

already knew what questions to ask. It was just a matter of finding the proprietor, which he did.

"Good day, sir. Do you remember talking with us?" Kenneth started. "We were through here a day or so ago and asked you a few questions about a coach and horses and you told us you had seen one almost fitting the description early in the morning. Said you thought it might be local, but you had never seen it before."

"Mistah, like I said before, I remember most who have been through these parts and I certainly told you I remember just as you said. And I'm sure of the time and the day," the innkeeper answered.

Things were beginning to come together in Kenneth's mind. Maybe, just maybe, John had experienced trouble on the way and had to make an unplanned stop. Maybe something had happened to the carriage or one of the horses. It was not likely, but it was possible.

"Sir, can you possibly tell whether or not you saw the same horse and carriage two days later going back south?" Kenneth pointedly asked.

"Well mistah, I reckon not. I wasn't here on the day you talking about but for a short while. I had to go off for a time to talk to folks who had been complaining about what took place at my inn a few nights before. It's likely lots of folks came through while I was gone... and the boy I have helping wasn't here, so I had to shut the doors for a while for several hours during the middle of the day," the innkeeper answered in a disgusted tone. He was upset because he had to take time away from his inn to address the complaint to the church elders.

Thwarted again, Kenneth looked with disappointment at Howard and both shook their heads.

"Mistah Hagins, we appreciate it. You have helped us

a great deal," Howard told the inn keeper with sincerity in his voice.

The two looked at one another again as Kenneth said, "I'm beginning to believe John had trouble on the way up and got delayed somehow. I don't recall any weather at home which was bad on his way up. I don't know whether the storm we got hit with also hit John on his way back. It wasn't much of a storm. It was a full moon, so they might have even traveled at night to get back. It will all come together, but it just don't make complete sense at the moment."

Kenneth was not only one of the best investigators anywhere to be found when it came to gathering hard evidence, but he also had the extra sense of intuition. If there were answers, he would know.

"Let's check every place along the way one more time. We know he never got back as far as Lancaster. You got any suggestions?" Kenneth asked Howard.

"You know something, I think we oughta stop at the not so fancy inn with the big man. He was awful nice, but he didn't seem to want to talk too much. Not saying he knows anything either, but we might find out a little something," Howard responded.

"I think you're right. We need to stop there. Wouldn't hurt at all. Don't reckon John stopped at any of the plantations on his way, do you?" Kenneth asked Howard.

Howard responded, "Not likely. He had his trip planned well, and we can get all the cotton from around Camden. It's just easier picking there and the fields make more than around here."

♦

Forty-five minutes more traveling and the men came upon Milt Chaney's Tavern. They dismounted, tied their horses to the hitch rail, and started up the front steps to the inn. They didn't see or hear anyone around so they stopped, stepped back off the porch, and decided to look around the south corner of the building. Off toward the wood line, they heard the striking of an anvil adjacent to what looked to be a set of stables big enough to house three or four horses. They continued toward the sound until they came upon the same huge man they had talked to on their way to Charlotte.

He looked up, a bit startled and asked, "How might I help you gentlemen?"

Again, Howard and Kenneth were amused how such a big brawny almost backwoods-looking person had such excellent command of the English language.

Kenneth asked again about whether or not he had seen a carriage on its way either north or south which fit the description of John DeMars' carriage.

"As you can see mister, I spend a considerable amount of time away from the inn and the road. There are all sorts of carriages and wagons traveling through here. I don't see most of 'em at all," Milt stated emphatically. "I wish I could be of help to you."

"Much obliged to you, sir, for what you have told us," Kenneth stated as he looked at Howard and said, "Partner, I think we might as well ride on toward Lancaster. We might make it there before dark if we push a little."

After they had mounted their horses and were out of earshot of Milt Chaney, Howard looked at Kenneth and asked, "Don't you think we needed to ask him more questions?"

"I think we learned a lot more than you think back there. More than you might know right now," Kenneth responded.

"What are you saying? I don't see your point," Howard said in a confused tone.

"Didn't you see the horse in the small pasture behind the stables?" Kenneth quizzed Howard.

"No, I think my view musta been blocked a bit," Howard replied.

"I think I saw a red horse of considerable size, say one almost the same size and pulling ability of John's horses," Kenneth stated.

"What you gettin' at? What's a red horse got to do with.....uh huh, my man, I think you might have something. I remember what the man said at Belair about the white horse and the red horse. Chaney admitted he might rent a horse or two to a man with a problem. He has stable's there for a reason and he probably shods horses too. I think you're right. But why didn't we ask him those questions?" Howard asked.

"Think we have all we are gonna' git from him and besides, didn't want to fool with a man strong enough to break an anvil," Kenneth half laughingly told Howard.

Lancaster was only a few more hours away and the two needed a rest for tonight and to plan tomorrow's strategy. Both were experiencing an ominous foreboding - *this was not going to be an easy investigation at all.*

CHAPTER THIRTEEN

Visit with Sheriff Haile the 1st
1852-1854

Kenneth and Howard bunked in for the night. Maybe a good night's rest would let a number of things come together. Possibilities were swirling in Kenneth's mind about what might have taken place. In ninety-five percent of all the cases he had ever worked, most of the pieces fit into the puzzle without much of a twist to it. But his intuition told him this case was more than likely going to be in the hardest five percent to solve; maybe it was going to be in the top one percent of the most difficult to solve.

Nevertheless, he had formulated a plan of action and his plan involved the local authorities. In this case, it was the sheriff.

Breakfast was excellent and both ate their fill. It was going to be a long day and the extra food would give them enough energy to make it through until noon.

"Howard, we need to find the sheriff. He ought to be around the courthouse on Main Street. I think we went right by it on the way north," Kenneth advised Howard.

"I believe you are right," Howard replied.

"I speck we can find out about our man at the tavern. Maybe the sheriff might know something," Kenneth told Howard as they rode off in the direction of the courthouse and jail.

Shortly after arriving at the jail, Kenneth and Howard dismounted, tied their horses, and went inside. There they found a deputy cleaning his gun.

"Excuse me, sir," Kenneth spoke in his gentlemanly

manner. "Are you the sheriff of the county?"

"No sir, I'm the chief deputy. Matthew Shaw's the name. How might I be of assistance to you?"

"I'm Kenneth Hattaway and this is Howard McTeer. We are working on finding a missing man, coachman, and team of horses and carriage. We know they passed through these parts less than two weeks ago."

"And you think they might have gone missing in these parts?" the deputy questioned back.

"Well, we're not 100 percent sure they disappeared in this county, but we have real strong suspicions they disappeared here. We are thinking they might have gone missing in the area up toward Belair," Kenneth stated confidently.

"And what makes you so certain you are right about where they disappeared?" the deputy questioned again.

"Well, sir, we traced the coach and man to Charlotte. He left there headed back to Camden. We can't trace him any farther south than the upper part of your county," Howard now spoke up.

"Are you sure he didn't disappear in Charlotte or nearer there?" Matthew asked again.

It seemed to be the beginning of a battle of the deputy against Kenneth and Howard, but Kenneth knew it was not. In fact, he realized he had come across a good lawman. He welcomed each joust from the deputy. It showed the lawman was interested and wanted to get what facts he could and make sure whatever he was told was solid information.

"Sir, we don't know exactly where he disappeared, but we are suspecting it was in your county. I'm an experienced investigator and I think I might be able to argue about where he vanished," Kenneth now stated with more certainty.

"I guess you have evidence to make such a claim?" the deputy asked pointedly.

"Like any good investigator such as yourself knows, you start with suspicions and go from there," Kenneth replied in a softer tone.

"And you'd be right there," the deputy replied. "Now let's talk about why you think your man and his driver when missing in this county."

Although the deputy appeared to be a noticeably sharp individual, Kenneth was a little skeptical about taking the discussion further. But at the same time, he didn't want to offend the deputy. He would like to be sure he would be on the same footing if he ever talked to the sheriff.

Almost as if the deputy was reading his mind, "Mister, I know you might be a little less likely to tell me what you know, but I can tell you for certain... whatever you need to say, you can say it to me. The sheriff and I go back a long way to growing up together. He'd trust me with anything he's got. So whatever's on your mind, you can say it to me. As we speak, I will tell you... the sheriff's gone up to the area you were talking about to look into another slave disappearance. You got two or three plantation owners up there who swear somebody's stealing their Negros. I speck I'd run away too. But they say they treat their Negros good enough so none of 'em would run away. I don't know whether they do or not," Matthew said.

"Do you think maybe there is a criminal element in the area up there?" Kenneth was quick to question.

Maybe his hunches were even more correct than he thought.

"I don't rightly know; there's not been much to complain about until recently. If something is starting up, I just don't know," the deputy responded. "We are going to have to see. The sheriff ought to be back tonight or tomorrow. He's a pretty smart fellow. He'll have ideas about what's going on."

The deputy seemed unusually open and honest with the two. Maybe it was out of respect for another professional. For whatever reason, he felt comfortable discussing matters with Howard and Kenneth.

"Tell you what. You need to write down all the particulars about this man DeMars, you said his name was, and I'll make a record of it and any other information you got to offer. Where did you say you two fellas were from? This man DeMars, he must have been an important man? I'll see to it the sheriff gets the information," the deputy said convincingly.

With the offer, Kenneth wrote down as much information as he thought necessary about John DeMars and where he or Howard might be contacted. Kenneth felt he had accomplished something but was still uneasy about mentioning Milt Chaney as a man who needed to be investigated. He felt he might talk about Chaney at a later date. He definitely would pay another visit to the Belair area and the sheriff's office, maybe even more than one.

"Deputy, you have been more than generous with the information. We are mighty obliged to you for it. I guess we had better be headed on our way back to Camden.

You'll see the sheriff knows about our inquiry?" Kenneth asked as if to be sure.

"Mister, you gentlemen can be sure I will make all this known to the sheriff. We'll keep a record of it and we'll contact you directly if we have any new information to tell you," the deputy stated.

♦

As the two men left Lancaster, their thoughts now turned to what they might report to Mrs. Alice.

"Howard, we need to talk and come to a consensus as to what we are going to tell Mrs. Alice. You know she is going to want to know every little detail about what we have found out. She is going to ask us pretty tough questions," Kenneth told Howard.

"I know exactly what you are talking about," Howard responded.

"I think it best we not tell her about our suspicions. She'll be wanting to go up there and confront Chaney herself. No, we don't need to upset Mrs. Alice more than she is naturally going to be anyway!" Kenneth continued.

"We are going to have to get our stories together and be consistent in what we are going to tell her and what we are not going to say!" Howard stated emphatically.

The two talked over their stories and by the time they reached Camden, they had perfected exactly what Mrs. Alice should hear and more importantly, what she should not hear.

Kenneth Hattaway had no intentions of anything less than a perfect presentation and one Mrs. Alice would accept, at least for the time being.

CHAPTER FOURTEEN

The Second Visit to Lancaster County
1852-1854

Kenneth Hattaway knocked on the front door of John DeMars' residence and was met by Mrs. John DeMars, who often answered her own door even though it was unusual for a Southern lady.

"Mrs. Alice, how are you today? I came by to see you at the request of Mr. Hayne Herndon. He said he would inform you of my planned visit," Kenneth said with upmost courtesy.

Alice DeMars knew Kenneth Hattaway because he and John had hunted many times together.

"Won't you come into the parlor and have a seat? May I offer you a drink?" Mrs. Alice was always considerate of her guests.

"Yes, ma'am, I'll come in and a glass of good water would be sufficient, thank you. I guess Mr. Herndon also told you the purpose of my visit," Kenneth said politely.

"He did, Mr. Hattaway. He informed me yesterday. I was hoping you might have information about my husband's disappearance," Mrs. Alice spoke with doubt and a bit of hope in her voice.

"Well, ma'am, we did go to Charlotte, and we can tell you... Mr. John did meet Mr. Pigg and the two of them struck a deal to use cotton Mr. John would provide. We are sure of the visit and the deal. Mr. McTeer verified Mr. John's signature on the contract. Now, what we don't know is what happened to Mr. John after he left Charlotte on his way home. We just don't know any details about what might have happened," Kenneth told her in the most pleasant tone of voice as he possibly could under the circumstances.

"You say you are positive he got to Charlotte and you say you don't know what happened to him on the way back?" Mrs. Alice asked.

"Yes, ma'am, we are sure he was on his way back... We also talked to the sheriff of Lancaster County - well, to his deputy. Now he seems like a smart man!" Kenneth exclaimed, knowing the next question would surely be Mrs. Alice asking why they did not talk to the sheriff himself. "We plan to go back and talk with the sheriff directly when he comes back into town and we also plan to do a lot more investigating up in Lancaster County."

"Well, I should think so," came the reply from Mrs. Alice. "Did you talk to anyone who had seen my husband along the road?"

"Yes, ma'am, but the man we talked to had seen your husband on the way to Charlotte, and we already know he made it there. Mrs. Alice, I will promise you... we will leave no stone unturned and we won't rest until we know what happened to Mr. John," Kenneth tried to convince her.

"I have a great deal of confidence you will do as you say, Mr. Hattaway. I don't doubt you in the least," Mrs. Alice said as she rose from her chair.

Kenneth stood as well and apologized for her plight, made his way to the door, and bid Mrs. Alice a good day as any Southern gentleman would do.

♦

As Kenneth rode away, he was more determined than ever to find out exactly what had happened to John DeMars. He made his way back to his office at which point he decided he would pick the best man on his staff to accompany him on his trip back to Lancaster County. *The trip would be tomorrow.*

♦

At dawn the next day, Kenneth Hattaway and Truett Taylor saddled their horses and rode north in the cool brisk autumn morning toward Lancaster County. Truett Taylor was a man with many years of investigative experience. Kenneth already knew where his first stop would be. Maybe he was going to be straight forward with the sheriff about his suspicions. *Little did he know what a surprise lay in store for him.*

It was afternoon when the two men reached the jail house in Lancaster. Once again, Kenneth and his partner tied their horses and went inside to talk to the sheriff. This time, they found the sheriff at his desk looking at papers and sipping a cup of coffee.

"How might I help you gentlemen?" the sheriff asked as he looked up at the two men entering the room.

"Are you the sheriff?" Kenneth asked.

"I am. I'm Baron Haile. Most fokes around call me Barry from when I was a chap. Who might you gentlemen be?" the sheriff asked.

"I am Kenneth Hattaway and this is my business associate Truett Taylor. We are private investigators from Camden. A couple of days past, I talked with your deputy Matthew Shaw about a missing man named

John DeMars."

"Yes, my deputy told me about you coming by and we discussed the case of your missing man. He tells me you think he went missing in the upper part of our county," the sheriff responded.

"Sheriff, we believe he went missing on his way back from Charlotte. We are not absolutely sure, but we are beginning to believe he might have disappeared up in the Belair or Twelve Mile Creek area," Kenneth responded.

"What makes you think he disappeared there?" the sheriff asked.

"Sheriff, I think I can be confident anything I say to you will be held in strict secrecy. Am I correct in my assumption?" Kenneth asked.

"Mister Hattaway, you can tell me anything you like and it won't go out of this room," Sheriff Haile expressed to Kenneth Hattaway.

"Well, we got suspicious about a feller we talked to up there who runs an inn. We asked him pretty straight forward questions any man would have had the courtesy to answer. He didn't seem to want to tell us the least thing. Seems like he got uncomfortable when we were talking. My instincts tell me he might know more than he wants to talk about," Kenneth said to the sheriff.

The sheriff raises an eyebrow, turns his head with a little smirk in his face and says, "Exactly who are you talking about?"

"The name on the inn is Chaney. We don't know any more about him than his name and he wasn't real friendly. He's a big fella with a beard. Seems to be plenty smart enough. Talks good and looks to have a pretty good business," Kenneth replied.

Sheriff Haile gave a halfhearted but serious laugh, took a deep breath, looked like he didn't want to talk, but started anyway. "Mister, for the first time since I became sheriff, we seem to have an unusual number of run-a-way Negros up there. Looks like they just disappear from the plantations. Nobody seems to know how they git gone. Don't see no strangers around. Don't have no troublemakers in the county. It's a mystery to us. Only thing we can figure is... we got us a local man who is stealing 'em... and probably has to have help. Now who's responsible, we don't know 'cause he or they is as slick as anything I have ever seen. Them Negros just vanish into thin air."

"Well, you say he or they have to be pretty smart, do you sheriff?" Kenneth implies as he thinks of how articulate the inn keeper was. He seemed to have enough intelligence and skills to do any number of things. Exactly what was he capable of doing? Was it possible it had come together so simply? Well, it seemed so at the moment.

"Sheriff, do you have any suspects you can talk about?" Kenneth pointedly asked.

"Well, I do, but I'm not real sure if I can pin anything on anybody. Got my suspicions, but it's all I got," the sheriff replied. "Seems like our man Chaney might know a lot more than what he's telling. We might be onto the same feller, but we got to have more on him than any of us have got now."

"So you think it's possible Chaney might be involved in things he ought not be involved in?" Kenneth questioned the sheriff.

"Like I said before, I got my suspicions, nothing more," the sheriff replied.

For Kenneth Hattaway, this was all he felt he needed to set a trap to find out if Milt Chaney had anything to do with John DeMars' disappearance and he planned to do it. Even as he was leaving the sheriff's office, things were beginning to come together much better in his mind.

The two investigators thanked the sheriff and promised to meet again and share any information they might uncover. The sheriff had been generous in his promises as well.

Maybe the efforts of the group would solve the mystery of John DeMars' disappearance and answer other questions as well.

♦

It was late in the afternoon when the visit with the sheriff concluded. The early start, the long ride, and the discussion with the sheriff had made for a tired couple of investigators.

Truett Taylor was usually quiet until he started to ask questions – at which point, his personality of persistence and seemingly endless *nit picking* questions would often overwhelm the strongest suspect's resistance. It was the main reason he was well compensated by Kenneth Hattaway. Kenneth saw a big role for him in this part of the investigation.

Kenneth and Truett found their way to a nice inn in Lancaster to board for the night. They felt tomorrow was going to be a long day. They had to eat, plan what they needed to do, and get a good night's rest.

CHAPTER FIFTEEN

The Re-Visit to Chaney's Tavern
1852-1854

The sun had not yet risen, but the two investigators were stirring. It was a three hour or so ride to the place they most wanted to visit. They had decided not to be confrontational if they talked to the man Chaney. Truett Taylor even agreed to tone down the manner in which he asked questions. A workable plan had been set.

Finally, they were on their last hill before they reached the tavern. They stopped short of the tavern at the spring which came from the rock. They could refresh themselves and their horses there. They could also go over their plans once again. Truett Taylor was warned by Kenneth Hattaway that Chaney's intellect was far superior to any ordinary backwoods man. Both men would need to be careful as to how they handled themselves when they confronted Chaney.

♦

As they neared the inn, the sound of a hammer on an anvil rang out. Perhaps Milt Chaney was blacksmithing in the shed at the rear of the inn. They dismounted, tied their horses, and walked the last hundred feet or so to see who was there. They were in luck. It was Milt Chaney hard at work.

He broke his concentration, looked up, recognized Kenneth, and asked courteously, "How might I help you gentlemen?"

"We are here to ask you about your services. We are going to be making cotton shipments through these parts up to Charlotte. We need to know if we might be able to get wagon services from you in case we break down or have trouble along the way. Last time I was here, I noticed you seem to have a pretty good shop," Kenneth said in such a tone as to be as complimentary as possible.

"Well, mister, it all depends on what particular kind of help you might need. I can do repair work on wagons, but I don't keep many spare parts around if you have really big heavy wagons," Chaney responded.

"Most of our wagons won't be the huge ones because of the road conditions and fording the creeks. We mainly want the services of someone if we have repairs we can't manage ourselves," Kenneth stated. He wanted Milt Chaney to think he could be of help.

It was the beginning of setting up a dialogue from which Kenneth might get answers to questions without really asking the questions directly.

Truett Taylor began, "I'll bet you've fixed a good many wagons coming through these parts."

"I've helped a few people," Milt Chaney responded.

"I reckon you could even trade a horse or two if someone made you a good offer. Have you ever traded horses? Where do you get most of your stock?" Truett had begun his questioning. Kenneth signaled him with a raised eyebrow to back off a little.

"Mister, you're a might nosey. No, I'm not a horse trader. I have stock I might let go ever so often if someone is in need of a good animal or might be having a problem. I might get a good horse cheap on occasion, but I don't set out to trade like you say," Milt responded with a slight hint in his response he was becoming aggravated.

"We might also want to be beddin' down for the night when we come through here. You reckon you can handle wagon drivers and a few Negros all at one time?" Kenneth quizzed.

"Like I said, mister, I reckon I'll do like I always do when a wagon or two stops here. I bed as many as I can inside, and it all depends on whether or not they want to share a bed or sleep on the floor. The Negros can sleep in the stables or pull the wagons up near the shed and sleep in the wagons. We've done all kinds of arrangements," Chaney replied confidently. "Like I said, we can handle most anything. When do you think you might be sending your people up this way?"

"Should be soon," Kenneth replied. "You'll have feed and hay if we need it?"

"Like I said mister, I handle most anything," Chaney said confidently again.

"And if we were to have a problem with a horse along the way, do you think you might be able to rent us one for a while if we were to pay you well and give you good collateral?" Kenneth quizzed again.

"I reckon I could lone a horse or two, mister," Chaney said in a lowered tone of voice. He was beginning to get more perturbed at all the questions.

Kenneth realized they had gotten all the information they were going to get. He could piece together the tidbits in his mind to make sense of it all. The two told Chaney they were looking forward to doing business with him, bid him good day, mounted their horses, and on a hunch, rode off toward Charlotte.

♦

About a mile or two up the road, Truett asked Kenneth, "Well boss man, what do you think we accomplished?"

"Well, I'm sure of one thing. We can get good service from him and we won't have to worry about anything happening to any of our folks on the wagons if they stay there," Kenneth replied.

"I'm not sure of what you are saying. Do you think we only know we can be sure of the safety of our wagons?" Truett came back.

"No, what I'm saying is... Chaney knows why we were there. He's not about to let anything happen to any of our people while they are there or even near his property. I'm not saying how much he knows about what happened to John DeMars. What I am saying is... he's still a suspect! I don't know if he is working for somebody or working with somebody. He might even be a ring leader if there is anything going on – I definitely think there is something going on! I believe he is a smart man, an exceptionally smart man. We have a bigger puzzle here than I thought. It's not going to be easy to solve!" Kenneth told Truett with certainty.

"Well, what do you think we can do to find out any more?" Truett asked.

"It's the reason why we are headed north. Might find out something there." Kenneth said, which brought a questioned look to Truett's face and brow.

Hagins' Inn was the destination Kenneth had in mind. He had more information now, especially with the sheriff telling him about alleged Negro stealing in the area. There were things he might also ask locals near Hagins' Inn about the man named Chaney. All of this would need to be done cautiously. If Milt Chaney was part of a bigger operation, there might be people around who were connected to a criminal ring, if there was one. They would surely not hesitate to inform Chaney of what was going on.

♦

"Good day to you, sir," Kenneth addressed the first man he came to in the yard at Hagins Inn. "Can you tell me where I might find the manager this day?"

"I think he just went out for a spell," the man answered. "He should be back in a short while."

"Much obliged to you, sir," Kenneth stated as he continued onto the porch of the inn. He found a couple of comfortable chairs and he and Truett decided to sit for a while to take in the pleasant breeze and free their minds. The two sat quietly for about thirty minutes before Hagins showed up. Kenneth recognized him and he recognized Kenneth.

"How might I help you today, Mr. Hattaway?" Hagins asked as if the two were old friends. "I remember you from the other day. You changed your partner, I see."

"This feller's name is Truett Taylor. He is a friend of mine and we need to ask you about business dealings. Do you have a private place we might talk?" Kenneth asked politely.

"Of course. If you two gentlemen would step right this way, we have a little place where no one will bother us," Hagins responded. "Now what kind of business are we talking about?"

"Well, we're gonna be running wagons through here to Charlotte with loads of cotton and we were wondering if you might be able to accommodate some of our men in case we might need to bed down for the night?" Kenneth asked. "We want to be honest with you. We done asked the man at Chaney's Inn down the road if he could help and he made us a pretty fine offer."

"Mister, I don't know what to tell you. I don't doubt he'll bed you down and help you in a good way and I don't know what kinda men you have driving your wagons. I know he has liquor and I don't serve any. He sometimes has pretty shady characters around from what I hear. I ain't gonna swear to it being fact, but folks who go by there sometimes says things. I speck he can do your wagon work. He's a pretty good blacksmith from what I hear. Been known to have horses he lets people use. All I know is... we run a clean place here and treat people right. Don't have no rift-raft hanging around or visiting. So mister, you just have to decide on your own what to do," Hagins said in a business-like manner.

"Mr. Hagins, I appreciate your honesty, and I really think you are sincere. No doubt we'll keep you in mind when we start our shipments and we will do business with you. One more thing. We might have Negros on the wagons. Can they sleep near the inn in the wagons? Kenneth asked.

"Mr. Hattaway, we'll find a way to accommodate your Negros. We always find a way when the coaches stop here with a Negro coachman," Hagins responded.

"I have one more question. Might you have accommodations for two weary travelers for this night? Kenneth asked.

"I think we can find a bed for you two gentlemen," Hagins replied.

♦

Kenneth Hattaway was tired and knew Truett could use the rest as well, even though it was a couple of hours before dark. Things were beginning to click in Kenneth Hattaway's mind. He wouldn't need to ask any more questions of anyone. He would have to come up with sort of plan to get information about the goings on at and around Chaney's Inn. His investigator's intuition was beginning to tell him the odds of ever finding out exactly what had happened to John DeMars were building against him as each day passed. Milt Chaney just might be the ring leader of......exactly what, he didn't know. But if Chaney had committed crimes, he would commit more. He would do it because he felt he could and get by with it... and even worse, it might have become a way of life for him!

♦

"Well, where do you think we go from here?" Truett asked Kenneth.

"Well, partner, I'm not exactly sure what we are going to do. We need to piece this together in our minds and decide where we might go from there," Kenneth responded, "But for right now, we're going to find out where the enticing smell of chow is coming from. We need a good meal and a good night's rest before we head back to Camden bright and early in the morning."

"When we get back to Camden, I've got to tell Mrs. Alice something and I don't know what it's going to be," Kenneth said with a worried voice.

"Truett, we are dealing with a man unlike any I have ever dealt with before. Usually, people who commit crimes just aren't particularly smart. Most of 'em make blundering mistakes which give 'em away, and their mistakes make 'em easy to track down. This man is smart and I am beginning to believe he is evil to boot. I know he will continue his criminal ways and he will kill more people. He might even enjoy what he is doing. He feels like he's much smarter than the law and other folks around. He's thumbing his nose at people and I'm not sure why. But mind you, even the smartest ones make mistakes and most of 'em eventually get caught and have to pay for what they've done. Just when this man will mess up, I don't know, but he will!!" Kenneth said in a highly disgusted voice.

"What we gonna tell Mrs. Alice this time really troubles me because I just don't what to say or how to say it. I just don't know. This is the part of the job I don't like. I don't like it at all!" Kenneth continued in an agitated voice.

♦

Indeed, what could he tell Mrs. Alice? And was there an ominous warning to Milt Chaney in his speech to Truett Taylor?

CHAPTER SIXTEEN

The Newspaper Story
1888

Carter Bradshaw was a mere boy when his grandfather John DeMars disappeared. His fondest memories were of the two of them off hunting in the woods and fields. In the absence of his father, Carter's grandfather had taught him to shoot and had bought him one of the finest shotguns available. At times, they were inseparable. He always wondered what it would have been like to have been with his grandfather longer.

♦

"Bodies found in Lancaster County may Date Back to the 1850s."

It was a curious headline in the local Camden paper. The details mentioned an old tavern and inn near where the remains had been found. The reporter had stated with certainty... *"the local authorities thought the bodies could be those of travelers who had vanished as they ventured along the highway in upper Lancaster County. There was even the possibility the travelers could be connected to a particular inn where they might have rested for the night."*

Carter Bradshaw took a special interest in it. Was there a possibility of any of this being connected to the disappearance of his beloved grandfather? As he reread the details again to be sure of the facts, it certainly seemed as if it could be. It was, indeed, the road on which his grandfather was last seen. But could he do anything to be sure of his suspicions? After all, it had been over 30 years and a war ago since his beloved grandfather was last seen.

He knew they had searched for his grandfather. He had been told this by his mother Christie and his grandmother, Mrs. Alice. His curiosity was whetted to a sharp edge as he read more and more about the discovery of the bodies.

Should he run to his grandmother with the news? She had been sorely disappointed when the investigators, many years ago, had not been able to find out anything for certain about his grandfather. Was the man who was hanged responsible for his grandfather's disappearance? Thoughts were swirling through John Carter's head. What if it was? Could he find out?

Someone would mention the newspaper story to his grandmother. It would be best if he was the first. Also, whatever information she remembered, she could give to him, or would it just be too painful - opening an old wound?

Mrs. Alice was over the age of 80 now. Fine Southern ladies never reveal their true age. She had endured the hardships of the war. She had been the family strength when many in the family had been so adversely affected by the harsh realities the war had brought to them. She was a survivor. By re-establishing connections of old business/social friends of her and John, she had managed to get her husband's business thriving again after the devastating war.

♦

Carter tapped lightly on the door just before noon. Mrs. Alice answered the door and they embraced warmly. Each was glad to see the other. Carter visited as often as possible.

"Grandmother, let's go into the parlor and sit and talk for a spell," Carter suggested to Mrs. Alice. Before he held the paper up, he cautiously proceeded, "Grandmother, there's a story in today's paper about things which happened up in Lancaster County about 30 years or more ago. I knew you were going to see the paper eventually, so I decided to bring you a copy. I've done some deep thinking and I'm wondering, well... I was wondering if any of this might have anything to do with Grandfather's disappearance. I don't want to disturb you, but I thought you would want to know. I know you would not forgive me if I knew this and I was not the one to call it to your attention."

Puzzled by what he had just said, Mrs. Alice looked with a frown on her face at Carter and asked for the paper. "Let me get my glasses. I want to read what it says. I want to read every word!"

Mrs. Alice took the paper from Carter and read every line carefully as Carter looked on. She had shown a much different reaction than he had anticipated. Maybe there was much more resolve and determination about pursuing the mystery of her husband's disappearance than Carter had imagined!

"Are they sure this might be the same time your

grandfather disappeared!? How exactly did they know!? I know what the paper says, but do you think they are positive about the time!?" Mrs. Alice questioned intensely.

"Grandmother, they say they think the man who was hanged about the same time is a suspect in many of the disappearances. Seems like many who stayed at his inn or stopped there for a while might have been victims. I don't know for sure if Grandfather would have stayed there, but he might have. I just wanted to be with you when you saw the paper - before anyone else showed it to you," Carter responded apologetically.

Then, to Carter's surprise, "Carter, we must find out for sure if one of those bodies belongs to your grandfather! And we need to know if one belongs to James! I don't know how we can manage to find out, but if it is at all possible, we need to know!" Mrs. Alice stated in as forceful terms as a Southern lady can state. "You must take it upon yourself to find an answer to all of this!!"

"Grandmother, you know I've always done your wishes. You know I'll do my best to find what answers I can!" Carter promised his grandmother. "I will gather my thoughts and a good man, and we will start as soon as earthly possible!"

"But first, Carter, you must stay and eat lunch with me. I just happen to have your favorite dishes prepared and you know I won't take no for an answer," Mrs. Alice said in a pleasant tone, showing she was satisfied. She knew Carter would do his best. She also needed to change her thoughts; her eyes were beginning to glisten over.

"Grandmother, you know I never turn down lunch

with you," Carter agreed in a comforting tone.

They both enjoyed the meal and discussed the gossip happening around town and made other small talk.

"Grandmother, I must be on my way. I have things to do in the office and I have serious planning to do. I will tell you now, I may be away for several days. Don't you worry, I'll be careful and I will spare no expense and I will take every measure I can to find out about grandfather!" Carter promised his grandmother.

Mrs. Alice's parting words were, "I know you will Carter, without a doubt, you will."

♦

Was there a possibility of actually bringing closure to this decades old heart-wrenching mystery and family tragedy? What exactly were the real thoughts of Mrs. Alice about finding out about her husband's disappearance? Had Carter made a promise which was beyond his abilities to keep?

CHAPTER SEVENTEEN

The New Investigation
Late 1880s

Carter Bradshaw had been given his grandmother's blessings for a new search for her missing husband. He had seen in her eyes and heard in her voice a renewed hope there might be a final solution to this awful tragedy for which she had suffered so long. Carter Bradshaw knew he must not fail. He must plot a strategy and execute it to the best of his abilities. Whatever he had to do and however long it might take was of little consequence. He owed it to his grandmother... and his grandfather.

♦

Carter knew of the investigation his grandmother had initiated when Mr. John first disappeared back in the 1850s. He knew the original investigator, Kenneth Hattaway, was still alive. But, there were still two great obstacles with this - Kenneth Hattaway was now in his 80s and the original investigation had taken place over

30 years ago.

Kenneth Hattaway lived on the outskirts of Camden. He had lost part of his fortune to the war in the 1860s, as had many in the area, but he still had the financial means to live in a substantial degree of comfort.

Carter felt the best place to start would be with the man who would have the most information. Kenneth Hattaway had delivered his report to Mrs. Alice back in the 1850s and even after an extensive investigation, he had concluded he would not be able to determine what had happened to John DeMars.

But was there something Kenneth Hattaway had never told John DeMars' family? Were there ideas he never explored? Carter felt he had to talk to the man if for no other reason than to get ideas and advice from him as how to best conduct a new investigation.

◆

The knock on the door was soon answered by a now bent elderly man who recognized Carter and smiled as he invited him in. Carter saw a copy of the same newspaper he had shown his grandmother, on Mr. Hattaway's desk, as he entered the home.

"I know what you're here about," Kenneth told Carter with a half-smile. "And I think you're on to something. I think what was written in the paper could, with little doubt, concern your grandfather's disappearance."

Carter was not expecting something so profound from Kenneth Hattaway. Instead, he thought he might have cautioned him against getting too excited about one of the bodies belonging to his grandfather.

"Mr. Hattaway, what makes you think my grandfather

could be one of those who were found?" Carter asked as they both took a seat in the sitting room.

"Well, when we first went on a trip years ago up into Lancaster County and talked to the folks around, we suspected the man who owned the tavern – Milt Chaney. He never did quite come across right with me or any of the others when we talked to him. We had suspicions from the onset, but we couldn't tell your grandmother or anybody else. We kept in contact with the sheriff in Lancaster County long after we told your grandmother we were probably never gonna find out what happened to John. If we'd told her differently, it would have done her no good. If she had known we suspected Chaney, she'd gone up there herself and confronted the man. Such would not have been good," Kenneth said with force he had left in his voice.

"Mr. Hattaway, I think you are right. My grandmother would've gone up there," Carter agreed.

"The man they hanged – Chaney - had a chance to confess his sins before they pulled the pin in the gallows, but he didn't. He didn't tell nobody anything. He was an evil man. I told my fellas and the sheriff up there he would probably kill again. He maybe thought he'd never be caught. It became a habit to him. Guess we know for sure now. Guess we got the proof!" Kenneth said in a somewhat disgusted tone.

"I think you are right, sir," Carter agreed.

"Exactly what you planning to do?" Kenneth quizzed. "You gonna try to find out about your grandfather, aren't you?"

"Mr. Hattaway, do you think I could rest if I don't try to find out as much as I possibly can?" Carter asked.

"I know how you feel, son. If I weren't an old man, I'd

probably saddle up with you and give it my best shot," Kenneth said with vigor in his voice.

"I wasn't expecting you to go, Mr. Hattaway, but I'm gonna be counting on you for advice and ideas about what I need to do first and I'll be wanting to know I can come back to you if I need more help," Carter said.

"You know your family can always count on me. I'll do anything I can to help you and I feel honored you are relying on me to give direction. The first piece of advice I'm gonna give you is to go see the present sheriff in Lancaster County and see what he knows from the sheriffs before him. Paper mentioned it was his granddaddy who helped hang the man who ran the inn where they found the bodies. I speck his granddaddy told him and his daddy something. Then you gotta go talk to the people who found the bodies," Kenneth declared in a highly interested manner.

"Mr. Hattaway, do you think any of the people who might have helped kill my grandfather are still alive?" Carter questioned.

"Son, I reckon most of them folks is dead for one reason or another. As much as I want to see you come up with something, you might just be wasting a lot of time and effort, but we both know you not gonna be satisfied til you try. You gotta try as best you can to find out whatever you can. And one more thing, son. I got most of the information we got scribbled down in old files. I don't know if they are readable anymore, but you welcome to 'em. This was personal to me, being your grandfather and I used to go hunting together. As a matter of fact, I think we took you on your first hunting trip down to the cabin on the other side of the river," Kenneth said reflectively.

Kenneth Hattaway went to one of his desks, pulled out old folders, brushed away some dust, and handed them to Carter.

"Son, I know you gonna have a tough time with this, but I admire you for trying. I just wish I could be of more help to you. This thing is something I have thought about over and over and it has bothered me for a number of years. Even in spite of the stupid war, I still can't help thinking about John. Your grandfather and me being such good friends and huntin' together and all. I couldn't bring myself to believe he could just disappear without a trace. I'm telling you - whoever took advantage of him had to do it while your grandfather was asleep. He was too sharp for it to happen otherwise. I'm sincere when I tell you to feel free to come back any time you see fit. Like I said, anything I can do to help, I will," Kenneth, with some vigor in his voice, told Carter.

"Mr. Hattaway, you have already been a tremendous help in more ways than you can imagine. My grandmother still thinks highly of you and we will forever be in your debt for what you have done," Carter stated sincerely.

◆

After the lengthy and much rewarding conversation had finished, the two bid good day and Carter Bradshaw was on his way back into Camden. He had many things on his mind and much to do. He now had more determination than ever to find out what happened to his grandfather.

CHAPTER EIGHTEEN

Back to Lancaster County
Late 1880s

The advice from Kenneth Hattaway, the still respected investigator, was well-heeded. Carter went to his place of business and sat at the desk his grandfather had used. He began to make a thorough plan of what he needed to do if he was going to have any success finding out anything about his grandfather.

Carter had been faced with formidable tasks before. He had left the Citadel in Charleston at the outbreak of the war and accepted a commission in the Confederate Army. He had been through some exceptionally bad times, but he had survived with courage and honor. This, too, would be a challenge worthy of a great honor if he had any measure of success.

◆

The planning had been done. He gave instructions to his second in charge as to how the business was to operate in his absence. He had selected one of the finest investigators from the firm Kenneth Hattaway had sold upon his retirement. Monday morning was the starting time for Carter's new adventure. He had no idea what the results might be or where it might lead him or how long they might be gone. Still, it was what he must do and he was looking forward to it with much anticipation.

◆

"Thomas, I hope you are going to stay with me. It might be a long time before we make it back to Camden," Carter told his companion Thomas Epps.

"Carter, we been friends for a long time. You know I'm gonna stick with you. I've never let you down before and I got no notion to do it now," Thomas Epps told Carter as he looked squarely in his eyes.

Indeed, Carter was positive Thomas would remain by his side just as he had during his days in the military. They had survived the war together and they would survive this ordeal together and no doubt do well.

Late in the afternoon on the first day, the two reached Lancaster. They took a room at one of the better local inns, dined, and turned in early for a good night's rest in anticipation for the long day ahead. The first stop tomorrow was the sheriff's office.

◆

It was a little after eight in the morning when they reached the county buildings where the jail was located. They dismounted and went into the sheriff's office.

"Good day, gentlemen, how might I be of service to

you?" a deputy cordially greeted them.

"Could you tell us where we might find the sheriff?" Carter responded.

"He's at the courthouse, but he should be back shortly," the deputy said politely. "Who might you gentlemen be?"

"Pardon me for my rudeness. This is Thomas Epps and I am Carter Bradshaw from Camden."

The sheriff walked in the door just as the Carter had finished his sentence.

"Good morning, gentlemen. How might I help you two?" Sheriff Haile asked in his usual manner. "I'm Baron Haile the Third; most people call me Barry."

"I'm Carter Bradshaw and this is Thomas Epps. Sheriff, we saw your story about the bodies found up in the Osceola area. If you have some time, would you be willing to discuss the matter further than what was printed in the newspaper?"

"Well, it all depends on exactly how much you gentlemen need to know. Now mind you, I'm not cutting you short or anything, but until I decide to investigate the matter further, I might not be able to tell you much more," the sheriff responded.

"Sheriff, do we have some place private to talk? I think you and I might be able to help one another," Carter responded.

Carter's words got the attention of the sheriff. He looked directly at Carter with a puzzled grin. "Just how do you reckon you could help me?" The sheriff motioned for the two to follow him to a small room. "Now, as you were saying."

"Sheriff, I'm thinking there's a possibility one of those bodies discovered might be my grandfather and another might be his coachman," Carter started.

The sheriff was now all the more interested. "Just how did you come to such a conclusion?" The sheriff was not doubting Carter, but was trying to be sure he had a good reason to make such a profound statement. He felt this was simply too much of a stroke of coincidence to be true.

"Sheriff," Carter began, "I have had the privilege of knowing one of the men who knew your grandfather. Seems the two of them talked at length about the goings on in the 1850s in your county. As I recall, he told me he believed, like your grandfather did, the man named Chaney could possibility have been the man who was a criminal ring leader. Seems as if nobody could ever prove anything against the man besides Negro stealing. I think Negro stealing was why they hanged the man, am I correct?"

Sheriff Haile looked up in disbelief, not able to say anything for the moment. What had he just heard? Someone had walked into his office who shared a common desire to solve a mystery which had haunted him since he was a youngster. He had always wanted to vindicate his grandfather for the crimes he had not solved. His grandfather had been one of his idols.

◆

Had fate re-dealt another hand which might be played successfully this time? Then again, neither of the two was so foolish as to believe anything from this point forward was going to be easy. However, there was a common interest with means and determination.

◆

"Seems to me you have done some investigatin' already," the sheriff responded with a smile.

"Yes, sir, I have and I'd be much obliged for any more information I might get from you about what your grandfather knew and what you have come across in the present time," Carter said hopefully.

"Mister, we might need to have a long talk. We can share what each of us knows. You can bring your fella along and I'll bring my deputy. I need some time to get what I got together," the sheriff stated as though he was suddenly delighted about his good fortune, "I've been looking through some of my granddaddy's papers, but I didn't have a chance to put any of it together. Lucky to have any of it at all. The Yankees burned part of the jail before they were driven out of town, but granddaddy had taken lots of his personal papers and some other things home and most of it got spared."

"I understand, sheriff. I know you weren't expecting someone to walk in as we did. I brought some of the information I have from the original investigation which was conducted. I hope it might be of help," Carter stated. "Sheriff, I'd like to see where the bodies are buried, if I could. I know there might not have been much left of 'em, but I would at least like to see the place if it is at all possible."

"Mister, we put each set of remains in a box as best we could and gave them as decent a burial as possible," the sheriff said. "Problem was, it had been a long time and they had been buried in just the dirt. Can't rightfully say we'd know who was who if we dug 'em back up."

Carter shook his head in agreement and said, "I understand."

Carter had hoped he might be able to eventually retrieve his grandfather's remains, but now he wasn't quite so sure. He would still hold out hope. Perhaps his grandmother might know some unknown characteristic of his grandfather not revealed to anyone else. Maybe something might show up in the bones.

"I can have my deputy show you out to the site where they was buried and I can get to work here piecing together what information I got," Sheriff Haile said.

"Thank you. It would be much appreciated, Sheriff," Carter responded politely in anticipation of what was about to happen.

"Now I have to tell you, it ain't no fancy place they are buried. We had to put them where nobody might grumble about some unknown body being in their burial ground. But like I said, we gave 'em a decent burial. Shore was better than what they first got," the sheriff said apologetically.

"Sheriff, I know you did the right thing by them," Carter told him, "I'm mighty thankful someone took the time and trouble to see they had a fittin' burial."

Carter and Thomas, along with the deputy, mounted their horses and the deputy told them, "If you will follow me, it's about 20 minutes away."

◆

The deputy was correct. No doubt he had made the ride many times before. The place they came upon was not the best cemetery Carter had seen. It was off in a remote area. There had been some attention paid to it, but not a great deal.

They dismounted near a tree and followed the deputy

to a specially marked site which had been set aside a short distance from the other wooden markers in the area. The sheriff had made a fairly good attempt to make a special place for the bodies they had brought in from the tavern site. However, it was still in a pauper's burial site. Carter was reluctant to ask who all might be buried there.

"As you can see, it ain't the best place to respect the departed," the deputy told Carter and Thomas, "but we gotta do what we can afford. The sheriff's a good man and would do better if he had the money and the help."

"I feel sure he would," Carter was quick to reply in a supportive voice. "No doubt he would; he seems like a good man."

The three men walked over to the distinctively raised places in the ground.

"Well, this is them. This is where we buried the remains. The sheriff had them blessed by a preacher and we showed them respect when we handled the bodies. We did the best we could do," the deputy stated. "We feel like some of 'em got a home now. I can't rightly tell you if one of 'em is your granddaddy or not. We pretty shore we got all the bodies the man had buried near the old place up there, but there might have been more he took off in the woods or did something else wit'. I hate to say it to ya, mistah, but it's somethin' you oughta know. And maybe he didn't kill no more. There's no way of tellin', there's just no way of knowin'," the deputy finished with an apologetic sigh.

"I appreciate immensely what you have done, and everyone I know will appreciate it as well," Carter replied.

Carter looked at the slightly raised mounds, each with a rock and a wooden marker with a simple *UNKNOWN* carved in the board used as a headstone. He wondered if one of them might be his grandfather for sure and if one might be James. He looked about and wondered what had really happened to bring his grandfather to this place, if he was in fact there.

After Carter had stood for a lengthy time looking at the mounds, he solemnly suggested to Thomas and the deputy, "I think we might oughta go."

Carter and the two others mounted their horses and began the short journey back to the jail. He already was beginning to think of what he might tell his grandmother about the burial site and what might have happened to his grandfather's remains. He was beginning to dread telling her about the dismal site. The newspaper story had mentioned the bodies had been buried, but the place had not been described. He knew she could never rest until she knew fully about the place. No doubt, Mrs. Alice would have to visit the grave site. She would have it no other way.

CHAPTER NINETEEN

New Information
Late 1880s

The ride back to the jail had been quiet among the three riders. Thomas felt he shouldn't say anything to Carter and the usually talkative deputy felt the same. So the only sounds were occasional snorts from the horses along with the clicking of horse hooves on the old road.

As they entered the jail once again, the men saw the sheriff had left a message saying he would return shortly. He had to attend to some unexpected business at the court house nearby, but he would be back as soon as possible.

Carter and Thomas walked into the small room where they had first been taken by the sheriff and sat down and began to discuss what they might realistically accomplish from their efforts.

Perhaps the reality of the situation brought about by the graveyard visit had deflated Carter's enthusiasm considerably. He still had hope the sheriff would have something in his store of information which might provide some satisfactory closure to the entire situation.

◆

Soon the sheriff returned and as he walked into the small room where Thomas and Carter were sitting, he started, "I've been thinking, and maybe, just maybe, we ought to ride up into the panhandle region this afternoon. We can catch some grub along the way and spend the night up there. While we got this on our minds, we need to go ahead and git started. We can ask around, if nothing else, then we can come back here, put what we get together with what we know already, and think about what we really can do. What say we give it a shot? You two, me, and my best deputy will ride up there."

♦

In slightly less than an hour, the four horsemen were saddled and ready for their trip to the Osceola area.

"Sheriff, do you think any of the folks who were around when all this crime took place might still be living?" Carter asked as they were riding along.

"Not real sure. There's some folks say old man Steele is alive and lives in the same place he always did. Nobody's gonna get anything out of him. I guess you heard about his testimony sending Chaney to the gallows," the sheriff replied.

"Yes, I talked with Mr. Hattaway about him in particular. Didn't know he was still around though. Thought he, like most of the others, was gone. The war and all, and time. Thought maybe we'd have to be mighty lucky to find anybody at all who might know anything," Carter said in a kind of discouraged tone.

"Well, we gonna go to the railroad people who first uncovered the bodies and find out if they know anything else or have come across anything," the sheriff responded. "Don't know if it will do any good at all, but you might want to talk to them. From there we can go up to some of the gathering places. I just haven't had the time to go up there and do any more talking with people. We got to hold out 'til we ain't got no more places to look."

♦

After noon, they reached the railroad camp. It hadn't moved as far as the sheriff thought. The creek bottoms down from Osceola Hill needed more rock and fill dirt than was originally thought. A crew to build a bridge across the creek was camped there now with wagon loads of timbers.

The railroad foreman O'Donnell had gone a couple of miles on toward Waxhaw to see what troubles might be ahead. The sheriff asked one of the men at the campsite about O'Donnell and was told he might be gone the entire afternoon.

"Well, maybe we can catch him on our way back through," the sheriff was saying when a horseman appeared not too far off in the distance.

It looked to be O'Donnell, so they waited to be sure if it was or wasn't. It was, and it turned out to be an extraordinarily fortuitous decision.

"Good day, gentlemen," O'Donnell spoke in his customary greeting as he approached the group.

"Good day to you, sir," each said in his own way.

"What might I do for ye gentlemen today?" O'Donnell asked.

"We mostly just wanted to pay a visit and see how things was goin'," the sheriff stated. "I wanted you to meet two men who are interested in what you found at the old inn and tavern. This is Carter Bradshaw and Thomas Epps. They are from Camden. Seems Mr. Bradshaw thinks he might know one or two of the fokes who was buried there."

"Ye might know some of them, ye say?" O'Donnell

responded as he gave Carter a puzzled look, "How might ye know who is buried there?"

"We had a family member to disappear about the time all of the crime was takin' place and was thinking maybe it was too strange of a coincidence not to be connected," Carter spoke up.

"Ye might have a point there," O'Donnell replied. "Could be they are connected. How does any of this involve me?"

"We mostly just wanted to stop here and see how things was since we was in the area," the sheriff said in a cordial tone.

"Glad ye did. Don't know if this is of any good to ye, sheriff, but I went back by the old place where the bodies were and I saw a Negro looking around the old house. I don't think there was anything he might steal. But, I think he was the same man I saw shortly after we found the first two bodies when I was riding off to a house to inquire about who might be in the graveyard. Didn't say anything to ye when we first talked. It's been playing in my mind. I might should have said something about it," O'Donnell finally told the sheriff.

"Hmmm, just might be one of the local Negros hunting up some junk or whatever he can find to use or sell. No tellin' what people look for," the sheriff responded.

"Well, when I first met him on the road right after we dug up the first bodies, he acted real strange... like he knew something about what had gone on at the old place. Don't reckon he had been in on it, do you?" O'Donnell quizzed the sheriff.

"Not likely. Chaney had nothin' much to do with Negros other than stealing 'em and makin' believe he was trying to set 'em free," the sheriff laughed.

"This one seemed to not want me to tell anybody I'd seen him and he just disappeared until I saw him a couple of days ago. Just strange. He surely didn't want me to tell the old man on the hill I'd seen him," O'Donnell replied.

"What old man you talking about?" the sheriff asked in a highly concerned manner now. It seemed as though he was much more interested than just a minute or two ago.

"An old man with an eye patch who lived about three quarters of a mile from the old place where we were digging," O'Donnell said.

"Could be old man Steele," the sheriff blurted out.

Carter's eyes opened wider as he heard the sheriff's words. Maybe there was a lead there. Maybe the Negro was more important than anyone had thought before.

"You think we might go visit this man Steele and look for the Negro?" Carter asked the sheriff.

"Don't think it'll do any good to talk to old man Steele, if he's the one who does live in the old house. He ain't gonna say nothing, especially to a lawman. Finding the Negro might seem like an easy job, but ain't none of the other Negros gonna tell who he is or where to find him. They fear the law and them who think they is the law too much. Can't say as I blame 'em. Only way some of 'em can stay alive or not get beat unmercifully," Sheriff Haile said apologetically.

"I guess you are right," Carter agreed as his voice sank. "I'm afraid you're right."

Carter had witnessed first-hand how Negros had

been treated after the war.

"Might there be anything else you've come across since we last talked?" Sheriff Haile asked O'Donnell.

"Other than what I just told you, ther's nothing to say," O'Donnell responded.

"Appreciate all you done for us. You did right by coming to us when you found the bodies, Yes,sir, we appreciate it," the sheriff said to O'Donnell.

With a head nod, the four horsemen bid farewell and were off in a northern direction,

Abruptly, the sheriff pulled the reins on his horse, and the other horsemen followed suit. "You know, I'm thinking maybe we need to look for some of the old timers around. Some of them might've remembered somethin' they heard or know just a little somethin'. Maybe if we go to Belair and start asking around, some old timer might just remember a thing or two."

Sheriff Haile the Third knew he was wishing and hoping more than he ought to be, but he was willing to try anything he thought might have the slightest chance of providing any information. Whatever little bit more he knew would bring more relief to his mind. Like Carter, he felt he owed it to his own grandfather.

CHAPTER TWENTY

The Search for Answers Continues
Late 1880s

No doubt to Carter and everyone involved, there was strangeness to this. The sheriff wondered why O'Donnell had not initially given him the information about talking to the Black man along the road and the old man in the big house. Had he simply forgotten or was there another reason? Maybe he didn't trust the sheriff or he didn't want to be involved any more than he had to be. Then again, he seemed exceptionally interested in the whole of the situation. What were O'Donnell's true intentions? Another mystery, perhaps?

Maybe riding to Belair and talking to some of the old timers there might be fruitful. One thing for sure, no one would know until they tried.

Sheriff Haile the Third tried to recall all the names of the plantation owners in the area around Osceola about the time Chaney was hanged. He could remember some right offhand, but they were gone now. Maybe the folks he might find could offer more. It was all a shot in the dark, but they had to try.

◆

About three miles up the road from Osceola and shortly before Belair proper, the Wilson and Pettus store, as they called it, had been built alongside the road. It had a stock of goods and supplies for those with smaller farms who now lived in the area after the big plantations had been broken up after the war. The labor had been freed and the plantation owners could no longer survive as they once had.

♦

The Wilson and Pettus store was just part of their joint business ventures. Across the road from the store, they had built a huge building to process cotton. They believed a cotton gin in the area would prove profitable and they were right. Even though the gin had just been put into operation, the wagons were backed up waiting to weigh in and unload their cotton to be bailed.

The Wilson/Pettus gin had the latest innovations of the day. They had contracted with a company in Georgia to deliver one of the finest machines made. It was to be powered with the latest in steam innovations. They had taken a considerable monetary risk in doing this, but there was simply not another gin so modern for miles and miles around. The farmers, large and small, would find it more economical to use this new imported gin rather than try to clean the cotton of seed on the farm.

The Wilson/Pettus gin also sold the cotton seed and hulls back to the farmers or others who might use them for feed or oil. They had planned out every angle and it looked as though their planning was proving to be highly successful.

♦

When the four horsemen came upon the people who were near the store and gin, they felt for sure they had a stroke of good fortune. Surely, among all the people they saw, there would be someone who might offer a sliver of information which might be useful. But there was a downside to it as well. Anyone who has ever talked to old timers knew some of the things they say are based on hearsay, so there would need to be *intelligent sorting* of the information. Nevertheless, hope was given a new chance.

The sheriff motioned to the others to pull over in a place not well noticed so they could talk about what they might do. He didn't want to scare people when they looked up and saw two lawmen with two strangers. Some were still suspicious about whether or not their property was going to be taken from them over a legal dispute an uncompassionate banker might call attention to. So they had a reason to be closed-mouthed to the law.

"Tell you what my deputy and I are gonna do. I think we are going to go on to Belair and let you two talk with some of the fokes here. Maybe let them think you are businessmen who are interested in 'em," the sheriff suggested.

"Well, I suppose I should be able to converse with them," Carter responded, "since I've been in the cotton business from the time the war was over. I would like to know what is going on up here in the cotton business as well."

The group split. The sheriff and his deputy rode off in the direction of Belair to the north.

Carter surveyed the crowd, looking intently for the older farmers. Hopefully, he might find an old timer and strike up a conversation which might prove fruitful. Thomas nudged Carter and cast his eyes in the direction of an older man with two younger boys. The two grey mules hooked to the wagon were up in their years as well. Thomas' intuitive nature told him they should talk to this man. He might know something of value.

Carter nodded in agreement and reined his horse in the direction of the wagon. The rugged old man looked up and said, "What can I do for you fellas?"

Carter, quick with a response to avoid suspicion, "Sir, I was just admiring your mules. I've always liked mules for working wagons. I'll bet those have been pretty good animals. How long you had 'em?"

"I ain't had 'em too long, but they is all I can afford. They was old when I got 'em. I speck they got a few more years in 'em. What you fellas business?" asked the elderly man.

"We're in the cotton trade and we were just looking at what was going on around these parts. Hope the folks don't mind. We're from down south of here in Sumter County. We was wondering just how well the cotton produces around here," Carter followed up.

"I tell you, mistah. If you get away from the red clay and rocks, it does fair to middlin, but hit don't grow like it do down south of here. Course, you might already know... beings you said you from way south of here," the stranger replied.

"Yes, most of the soil we are used to is the sandy black type and it grows pretty good cotton. Now exactly where do you farm?" Carter asked, hoping he might get an answer which would lead to more questions.

"We farm down in the Six Mile region 'bout a mile and a half south of here. Used to be some big plantations there, but most of 'em broke up after the wah was over and the slaves run away," the stranger answered.

"Have you always farmed in the Six Mile area?" Carter continued.

"We growed up right near thar and some of the family has been thar most of they lifes. The family got spread out and some got kilt in the wah," the elderly man answered.

"Did you ever hear of a farmer named Chaney from the Osceola region?" Carter asked anxiously.

"Mistah, I heard rumors about a man named Chaney who was hung in Lancaster, but I don't 'member much at all about him particular. They all said he ought to be hung. They was rumors about he'd kilt people, but I can't remember much about hit," the elderly man answered.

The excitement of the moment turned depressing for Carter. He knew, to the best of his reasoning ability, these few tidbits were probably the most he might ever get in the way of information from anyone, so he pulled Thomas aside and relayed to him the same thoughts.

Carter and Thomas looked carefully at the people waiting in their wagons and the others standing around and saw nothing but faces much too young to offer any good information of the olden times. They shook their heads with a sigh and jointly decided they might as well head north with hopes the sheriff might be doing better.

♦

Less than an hour's ride later, they saw the sheriff and his deputy and joined up with them and were informed the sheriff and his deputy had experienced no better fortune than the two had experienced at the cotton gin. All four came to the same conclusion. They might need a different strategy. But exactly what different strategy might they employ?

Carter began, "Sheriff, what about the man's family? Do you think it's possible we might find some of Chaney's family, if he had any children? Reckon his wife might have passed on, or maybe she could still be living."

"Don't rightly know if'n we could find the family. Seems his wife and chilren was forced to move on after the land was sold for taxes. Youda thought they might woulda had the money from his robbin' all them fokes," the sheriff stated confidently. "But I guess he hid it all or somebody else stole it while he was in jail. I think he had three youngins. Seems like I remember he had a boy and two girls. Won't be easy to find the girls, they'd done changed their names if'n they got married. I think his wife had moved back to North Carolina. Took the chilren with her. No tellin' if the boy changed his name to his mama's out of shame. They might have all been adopted by somebody or she remarried, I just don't know and I ain't hopeful much about ever finding any of 'em. I just don't know. Maybe we all might just stay up here tonight and head back to Lancaster tomorrow after some good food and rest," Sheriff Haile said.

Carter sighed as he looked at Thomas and asked him if he had any suggestions.

Thomas replied, "Short of finding the Negro that O'Donnell said he thought might know something or getting something out of the old man who might be Steele, I think we are at a dead end. The likelihood of finding the Negro and then getting him to talk is not good at all."

Carter spoke up, "I'm beginning to think the same. Maybe it was only a fantasy. I just hate to face my grandmother with the news."

"She'll understand more than you think. We're not done yet. We'll all feel better tomorrow," Thomas continued. "We'll all feel better after we rest."

♦

The night was not restful for Carter. The thoughts of his failure were not so troubling as were the thoughts of facing his grandmother and telling her about where he thought his grandfather was buried and how upset she would be. Would she ever believe any one of the bodies was her beloved husband anyway?

He drifted in and out of sleep. What might they have done differently? Had he initially been too enthusiastic? Might there ever be a chance he could find anyone who had any answers and was willing to talk? It seemed as though each question brought on another set of questions. Every new question lacked a satisfactory answer.

He decided one thing he would do for sure. He would visit Mr. Kenneth Hattaway again. He would have some advice.

There still might be something of interest in the files the sheriff said he had kept. Carter knew they would see them tomorrow. Then again, had he been too hasty in his assessment of meeting any people who might know something? Maybe so. Thirty- five years is a long time.

CHAPTER TWENTY ONE

"Grandmother, I Have Failed"
Late 1880s

The next morning, the four were up at dawn. They were ready to get a good breakfast at the Belair Inn and be on their way. It was a fairly long ride to Lancaster. They could study the papers the sheriff had and they could go over any ideas which might pop into their minds in the meantime.

They went by Chaney's Tavern again and they looked at it with questioning looks. How had such an insignificant looking place come to be so important in their lives and the lives of who knows how many others? What had really happened there years ago? The secrets seemed certain to be buried away when the last person who had any dealings with the goings on there was gone. *Were they all gone?*

Each of the four looked at one another as they paused, but said nothing. They pointed their horses in the direction toward Lancaster. They made their way down the slope past the railroad bed and up the other slope and didn't look back. Maybe each felt one more glance would only confirm a man named Chaney had thumbed his nose at them once again.

♦

Mid-afternoon came soon as the four riders had reached the jail. They dismounted and went inside, grabbed a fresh drink of water, and stared at each other with looks of frustration.

"Sheriff, do you think there is any way we might find the Negro whom O'Donnell saw at the old shack... and do you think he really knows anything worthwhile?" Carter asked the sheriff again.

"I can't rightly tell you if'n he does or doesn't know anything and if he would tell you if he did. We probably ain't gonna find him. They make themselfs scarce when they don't want to be fount. And like I said before, I don't blame 'em. If'n I was them, I'd do the same. I know... if they suspect the law, they gonna hide even better," Sheriff Haile replied.

♦

The remainder of the afternoon was spent looking over the papers in the office, talking, and making suggestions... and shooting down a few of those same suggestions. Carter and Thomas bid the sheriff and his deputy a good night. They had left with the understanding that *if anything new came to light or anyone else came to town inquiring about a missing loved one, then the sheriff would send a rider to tell Carter and Thomas.* The promise was sincere and it would be reciprocal.

◆

Thomas and Carter were up early the next morning. The ride was going to be long and difficult, not so much physically, but there was dread hanging over Carter because of what he knew he had to tell his grandmother.

Was it possible for him to talk to Kenneth Hattaway first? What if his grandmother found out he had not come directly to her upon arriving in Camden? He already had to disappoint her with bad news. It surely would only make matters worse. He knew in his heart he had to go first to his grandmother.

◆

It had been a full day's ride and the evening sun was setting as the two horsemen reached the outskirts of Camden. Carter could at least put off the delivery of the bad news until in the morning when he knew his grandmother had gotten out of bed and dined on her tea and fruit.

◆

Carter knocked gently on the door around ten a.m. As usual, Mrs. Alice opened the door, and smiling widely with what looked to be mixture of hope and tears in her eyes, reached out and grabbed Carter in her embrace.

"I am so glad to see you. Come in and have a cup of tea with me at the table and you can tell me what you learned about your grandfather," Mrs. Alice anxiously said.

Carter had to fight the feeling of wanting to run away. He was highly troubled with what he knew he had to tell his grandmother.

"Grandmother, we talked to the sheriff in Lancaster and we even went up to the area where we think

Grandfather might have disappeared. Grandmother, it has been a long time. Folks up there didn't seem to know much and I just hate to say it this way, too many of the people who were there thirty years ago are now gone. I hate to say it, but it's true," Carter said apologetically.

"Carter, I suspected such, and I didn't know whether or not we might ever know what happened to your grandfather," Mrs. Alice conceded.

"Grandmother, I feel as though I have been a failure. I feel like I have let you and Grandfather down when it counted most. We tried to find out all we could, but we just didn't find anyone who remembered anything about what had gone on. It's just been too long and the folks who lived then are gone and scattered, it seems like, to the four corners of the earth," Carter reiterated.

"Carter, I want you to tell me the truth. Did you find your grandfather's grave? If you did, I must go see it," Mrs. Alice said with a tear in her eye.

"Grandmother, I cannot tell you a lie. We found where they had buried the remains from the old inn. But grandmother, they don't know who was who when they buried them proper," Carter said hesitantly.

Mrs. Alice could tell that the tone of Carter's voice was not normal. What was he withholding from her? She was straight to the point.

"Carter, you must tell me where your grandfather is buried. I must know and I must go to his grave to see him!!" Mrs. Alice insisted.

"Grandmother, the trip will harm you greatly." Carter feared the trip might kill her and he certainly didn't want her to see her beloved husband's grave in a pauper's cemetery. "We cannot say for sure whether or not one of the bodies is Grandfather."

"Carter, you must take me to see the graves you talk about! I must stand over them! I will know if one is your grandfather and then we must get the remains and give them a proper burial! Your grandfather has a place all picked out for us. We must place the remains there! We must have a proper burial ceremony. I will stand for nothing less! We must go as soon as possible. I will know which grave is your grandfather!! We must also get roses. I want enough roses to put on all the people who are buried with your grandfather!!" Mrs. Alice pleaded.

Mrs. Alice had made her point and Carter knew he would have to abide by her wishes. Still, in the back of his mind, he could not put away thoughts of how she would react when they came upon the burial site.

"Grandmother, you have spoken and I am sure you will not rest until we have done as you wish. I will go directly and start planning for the trip. The roses will be picked shortly before we leave. We will have all the roses possible for the journey. Robert will prepare the horses and carriage for the journey and James's son will ride with us. He will want to know, too," Carter agreed.

"Carter, I have no doubt you will do what you say. You have not failed; you just don't realize what you still have to do and you will do it well. Carter, I am certain you will finish your mission!" Mrs. Alice told him.

Carter looked at the sincerity in his grandmother's eyes with a puzzled look in his own and stated, "Grandmother, you have always been right."

"Carter, we can pack a picnic to have along the way.

Yes, we will need a picnic lunch. We don't have to rush.
I hear Lancaster still has fine inns to stay at. We can
spend the night there. We will make it a two day trip. I
want to have plenty of time to spend at your
grandfather's grave!" Mrs. Alice said in a spirited tone.

"Grandmother, when you say you are ready, we will
go." Carter responded.

"Carter, we will go as soon as it is earthly possible,"
Mrs. Alice softly replied.

◆

Carter was convinced his grandmother's wish to see
the gravesite of her beloved husband had to be fulfilled.
He was relieved she had not wanted to go see the tavern
where John DeMars might have spent his last earthly
night. Mrs. Alice certainly didn't need to be put through
such an ordeal. Carter despised the thought of ever
seeing the tavern again.

CHAPTER TWENTY TWO

Visit to the Pauper's Cemetery
Late 1880s

Just as his grandmother had asked him to do, Carter prepared the best coach. James's son, James Jr., was also notified he was to ride with them. He and Carter would ride horses and Mrs. Alice and her maid would ride in the coach along with the flowers and the picnic. Robert, like all the other coachmen who had served the DeMars family over the years, was excellent. The ride would be as smooth as possible. They would stop along the way and eat and rest and get to Lancaster before dark. They could settle for the night at an inn and rise whenever Mrs. Alice wished and then go to the cemetery.

Carter would pay the sheriff a courtesy visit to inform him of their intentions. He also wanted to check with the sheriff to discuss any new developments, if, indeed, there were any.

Except for the delicious meal served at the picnic, the trip was uneventful and the group arrived at their inn before dusk. Carter made sure James Jr. and Robert were fed and had a place for a good night's sleep.

♦

The morning seemed to come earlier than usual. Even Mrs. Alice was up shortly after dawn. Perhaps it was the anticipation of seeing her beloved husband's grave and somehow knowing there finally would be closure to the many years of her wondering.

She would also have to now deal with the finality her beloved John's death. The hope of him miraculously appearing in her doorway after all these years had to be erased from her mind.

The ride to the cemetery was fraught with dreaded anticipation. The last turn in the old dirt road was negotiated and a short distance away was the edge of cemetery. It wasn't as bad as Carter had remembered. The cemetery looked as though someone had paid attention to it since his visit there.

◆

As Carter held her arm and guided her through the cemetery to be sure she would not turn an ankle, Mrs. Alice stopped and paused at the third mound in the area where Carter had said the graves from the inn were. Just as she did, a beam of light from the morning sun shining through the tall pines nearby touched her and the grave. She paused for a long time. Her eyes flooded with tears. Carter gave her a handkerchief to wipe them away. He gently took his grandmother's hand to steady her. He had felt her body weaken from the emotions of the moment.

Mrs. Alice wanted to talk, but choked on the words... Finally, she was able to state excitedly and tearfully with a break in her voice, "This is your grandfather!! Carter, this is your grandfather! I know it beyond any doubt. I feel it all about us. He is here. God has told us, he is here!!"

Carter was speechless. He held her hand tighter and looked slightly away so as not to let his grandmother see his eyes also filling with tears.

She reached down and placed several roses on *John's grave*. "James is next to him. I know for sure. Please have James Jr. and Robert place roses on the other graves. They cannot be forgotten! None of them should be forgotten. Have James Jr. come here to see his daddy's grave," Mrs. Alice stated in a subdued voice.

"Carter, you must do whatever it takes to get your grandfather's remains out of this awful, awful place!! You must also get James's remains. I cannot live with the thought of your grandfather being here! He must have a proper funeral and he must be buried in the place he had picked long ago! You must be sure his body is retrieved as soon as possible! You must promise me you will do as I wish!!" Mrs. Alice pleaded with tears flowing.

"Grandmother, I promise I will do everything earthy possible to ensure Grandfather is removed from this place. James's remains will be removed as well," Carter responded in a strong positive voice.

"You must keep your promise to me, Carter, even if it is after I am gone. You must see to it... so we can all rest!!" Mrs. Alice pleaded again.

♦

After a considerable time, the group left the cemetery and decided to head back to Camden. Mrs. Alice felt with all her heart, she had stood over the remains of her husband. Though she found comfort in it, she hurt with the absoluteness of knowing her husband was gone. Her only satisfaction now would be - she sorely believed her beloved husband's remains would be moved and placed in Camden. She could have comfort in visiting them as often as she chose.

♦

Carter had formidable tasks ahead. How could he ever convince the sheriff his grandfather's body was in the particular grave Mrs. Alice had chosen, or in any one of the graves? He also felt he had to give more effort to finding anyone who knew about how the people were killed. Surely there might be those who still knew something, but the thought re-entered his mind: *"it had been over 30 years ago and their efforts thus far had yielded barely a smidgen of evidence."*

♦

Carter knocked on the door of Kenneth Hattaway one mid-morning and was greeted again by the man who had initially searched for his grandfather.

"Come in, Carter. Tell me what you found out with your visit to Lancaster County. Did you have any luck?" Kenneth asked.

"No, sir, I think we were failures. I don't think we found out anything about solving the mystery. We did see where the remains had been placed," Carter answered in a dejected tone.

"Well, tell me what you did and why you think you didn't have any success," Kenneth said pointedly.

"Mr. Hattaway, we talked to many people and there's no one who knows much about the murders happening, let alone anyone who can recall exactly what did happen. Most of the folks we saw were younger. The older generation didn't seem to remember anything either. It was highly frustrating and downright discouraging," Carter stated in a dispirited voice.

"Carter, let me tell you what frustration is all about. Many years ago when your grandfather first disappeared, we thought we had found the man who had killed your grandfather. As a matter of fact, we were sure he was a criminal and had committed all sorts of other crimes. Even the sheriff at the time agreed. We just could not pin anything on Chaney. He was brilliant – in an evil sort of way. He had to have people who knew what was going on to help him. One man could not have done it all. The sheriff couldn't find nobody and I couldn't find nobody to blame. Solving a crime 35 years after it happened is many times harder than you want to think. You tried, and knowing you, I'm sure you are satisfied any further effort on your part would be futile or you would still be in Lancaster County," Kenneth said in a firm voice.

"I appreciate your confidence in me. Thank you, sir," Carter responded.

"Now what I would suggest to you is... you start working on ideas how to get the sheriff up there to release Mr. John's body, if you think it might be your grandfather, so your grandmother can have the slightest peace of mind. Getting the body released is not going to be an easy task. To tell you the truth, it may well be an impossible task. You and I both know we are not going to try to fool your grandmother in any way... and I don't think you will try!" Kenneth said emphatically.

"No, sir, I would never try to fool my grandmother. My conscience would not allow me to try to deceive her," Carter stated as he shook his head.

"One last thing. You need to get all the rest you can

and be around your grandmother as much as possible. She's like me, her days are growing fewer. Would you give her my love and tell her she is in my thoughts and prayers?" Kenneth said politely.

"I certainly will. I want to thank you again for all you have done all these years for our family," Carter said in the sincerest of tones.

The two bid farewell and Carter resigned himself to the idea he might never know the truth about his grandfather's disappearance. However, he knows with all his being, he has to do his best to retrieve his grandfather's remains. He also understands how difficult getting those remains is going to be.

CHAPTER TWENTY THREE

The Train Stop at Osceola
1889
Sebastian Wolfe

The village of Osceola had been surveyed just about the time the railroad had laid the tracks in the valley north of the hill. In fact, there was a railroad stop there now. People could hop the train for travel either eastward or westward. The little village had a post office, a general store, and other small businesses to serve the people nearby or those passing through. The water tank below the village and near the railroad track provided water necessary for the steam engines when they stopped.

But there was a big problem; so big in fact, it eventually led to the demise of the small village. No one had planned for the railroad being placed so deeply into the hill. No one seemed to want to spend the funds to build the necessarily high bridge strong enough to support loaded wagons between the steep banks the railroad had created.

Eventually, the main north-south road moved east of the village and Osceola dried up and died, but not before it played an almost unbelievably fateful role in one family's life.

♦

"Big George, what say we get off here for a spell? They're gonna take on water and get the mail and they'll be here about an hour. I remember camping out here a while back. Seems almost as it was yesterday," O'Donnell told Big George with a reminiscing voice.

"Sho nuff does boss man, sho nuff does. You knows we never gonna forget what we fount here, is we!?" Big George added as he shook his head, still in disbelief.

"Ye right big man. Looks like the old shack is still there. Thought they'd burned it or torn it down by now," O'Donnell said half laughing.

"It musta been an awful evil man to do all dem killings!" George said in a serious voice.

O'Donnell and Big George were passengers now on a train running on the tracks they helped build. They had taken a ride all the way to Monroe in the east and were returning to Chester in the west. It was part of a ride to see if there might need to be further work on the banks and hills along the right of way. It was a much easier task than the digging had been. The cool air blowing through the windows of the passenger compartment felt good.

When the train made a routine stop at Osceola to take on water, deliver and pick up mail and passengers, they had decided to stretch their legs a bit.

"Let's go see what the little village has to offer, big man," O'Donnell suggested to Big George.

"Mighty fine idea, boss man," George responded.

As they first approached the main road in the center of town, each thought there was not much to offer. They walked down the main street. They looked at the post office. There were people there. The incoming mail bag from the train had been delivered.

As they looked about in the direction of the general store, they noticed an elderly man sitting on a makeshift stool. He was fumbling with his pipe trying to get it lit. O'Donnell and George walked over to him and O'Donnell took a match from his pocket struck it and said, "Let me give you a hand old timer."

The man puffed twice, blew a small puff of smoke and said, "Th-thank yo-you, sir." He had a stutter to his speech.

O'Donnell was quick to respond, "You are quite welcome, sir. Are you from around these parts?"

"I-I li-live in a small ca-cabin down in the wo-woods from here," came the reply from the stranger.

O'Donnell looked at the vagabondish man and thought surely he was a drifter just passing through. He was wrong. Still curious, he asked the man anyway, "Do you ever travel much?"

"I-I be-been all over," the man responded.

"Just where have you been?" O'Donnell prodded.

"I-I bee-been to Ch-Charleston. I-I se-seen the ocean," the old timer said smiling.

"Ummh, interesting, and how might ye have traveled to have seen so much?" O'Donnell continued.

"Th- it wa-was many years ago. I-I hi-hitched a ride on wagons passing th-through these parts," the old timer answered.

O'Donnell was naturally fascinated with people and had always sought out characters such as the tattered clothed stranger because they seemed to have fascinating stories. Such was the case with this man.

"Do ye still travel much?" O'Donnell continued, thinking they had better get back to the train before it pulled out.

"I-I g-go when I ha-have a way to go. I-I ne-never ro-rode a train yet," said the stranger.

"Why not?" O'Donnell thought. He looked at Big George and evidently the two were thinking the same thing as they smiled back at each other.

"Tell you what I'm gonna do for ye. If ye want to ride the train, I'll let you ride to Chester with us and then I'll arrange for ye to come back here on the next train coming back. We'll even have our own special little space on the train," O'Donnell offered. He thought the stranger would probably turn him down on such short notice, and was surprised at his answer.

"I-I ca-can go ri-right now. I-I do-don't have no-body to answer to. I-I'd like to go," the stranger responded.

O'Donnell knew he had to follow through on his offer, so he asked, "Might you have any baggage to take with you?"

"I-I don't ha-have nothing 'cept wh-what I got on," the stranger replied.

O'Donnell thought to himself, "What have I gone and done?" He wasn't about to let the stranger down and he knew he had to make sure he was fed before he put him on the train back to Osceola, but he could do it now since he had a break in his work schedule.

♦

"By the way, if we are going to be riding together, I guess we should know who one another is. My name is Thaddeus O'Donnell and this gentleman's name is

George McAfee. Most folks call him Big George," O'Donnell stated.

"I-I am Sebastian Wolfe," the stranger replied.

"Good to meet you, Sebastian Wolfe. It's a pleasure," O'Donnell said as Big George concurred by nodding his head.

O'Donnell, Big George, and Sebastian Wolfe were soon on their way to Chester. The train whistle had sounded and the train was beginning to pick up speed.

"Well, what do you think about your first train ride?" O'Donnell asked Sebastian.

"I-I li-like it. Hits mu-much better th-than the best wa-wagon I ever rode," Sebastian answered with a grin as he took his pipe from his mouth.

"When was your first wagon ride and where did you go?" O'Donnell asked half laughing.

"I-I hi-hitched a ride from the ta-tavern," Sebastian answered.

The smile was gone from O'Donnell's face in a split second. He and George looked at one another and both saw the sharp change in the facial expressions of the other.

"You say ye hitched a wagon ride from the tavern. What tavern would it be?" O'Donnell asked in as reserved manner as possible under the circumstances.

"Th-the one th- where th-the railroad is now. Hit don't do business no-no more," Sebastian stated.

O'Donnell's interest in this man's conversation had become extraordinarily serious in just a few seconds.

"Now you say ye knew of an old tavern. Would it be the one and same a man by the name of Chaney ran?" O'Donnell questioned.

"Th- ri-right. I-I used to go th-there a lot and ride with

people when th-they left in th-the mornings. Some had go-gone fore I-I got there sometimes. I-I would go there ju-just before dark and tell 'em if'n I-I wa-was wanting to-to go the next day, but but sometimes they'd left fore I-I got there the next day," Sebastian laboringly stated.

"I wonder why they'd left so early?" O'Donnell sarcastically said out loud. He already thought he knew what had happened.

He looked at George, and George said without being asked, "I thinks you right, boss man."

"How many times did the people leave too early for you to ride with them the next day?" O'Donnell continued.

Sebastian was packing his pipe again and once again O'Donnell lit the sweet smelling tobacco. "Hit-hit wa-was more than a fe-few times," Sebastian answered.

O'Donnell asked, "Do you ever see any of the fokes who you knew from the tavern around the area where you stay?"

"Most most of th-the people are gone," Sebastian said with a sigh.

"Excuse us for a moment," O'Donnell said to Sebastian in a mannerly way.

O'Donnell stepped away and he and Big George talked at length. They wanted Sebastian to take in the wonders of his first train ride, so they decided to give him a break. They offered him a drink of water and food, which he was quick to accept. He ate as though he had not eaten in a while. Sebastian rested to let the meal settle as O'Donnell took a piece of paper from his pocket and wrote down the information.

O'Donnell saw Sebastian open his eyes after a short nap and the conversation was renewed.

"How was the meal and the nap?" O'Donnell started. "Seems you like the train?"

"I-I like the train," Sebastian replied in a relaxed tone with a boyish grin.

"Tell me, when you think about your times at the tavern, can you remember anyone who is still around who was around back then?" O'Donnell asked again, thinking the man might have a change of memory – he hoped.

Sebastian thinks for a while and finally answers again, "I-I can't think of no-nobody I know."

"What happened to all the slaves from the plantations around after the war?" O'Donnell asked, trying a new line of questions.

"So-some of 'em moved into the area a-around Van Wyck," came the reply from Sebastian. "So-some of them even moved down near th-the Indian Re-reservation."

"You sit back and enjoy the rest of your train ride," O'Donnell said as he broke off the conversation and motioned George to come over again.

"Boss man, I knows what you's thinking, and you's already knows I'm gonna go wif ya to look for da man you saw after we'd dug up them bones. Where's we gonna start?" George asked half laughing. "When's we gonna start boss man?"

◆

Had it been O'Donnell's intentions all along to search out answers to the mystery he and his crew had started? Or, could it simply be the coincidence of meeting Sebastian Wolfe had kindled his curiosity to the point he had to act. It had come at a curious time; he and Big George had time off before they were to start another railroad project. Was he thinking the Black stranger he had met might have sought safe refuge among the Negro settlements near Van Wyck or the Indian Reservation?

It was a tremendously long shot. Maybe he felt Big George's *abilities* were rubbing off on him.

CHAPTER TWENTY FOUR

The Trip to Van Wyck
Late 1880s

For whatever reason, Sebastian's words were the catalyst which spurred O'Donnell's hidden thoughts to action. It was now clear, more than ever - he and Big George must settle what O'Donnell felt they had started. Maybe the Irish blood in his veins had been set to a boil. Perhaps it was something far different. Exactly what it might be was of secondary importance now. The matter must be pursued as far as it would take him and his sidekick. Big George was the best man anyone could have as a partner for the immediate and long term mission. He could help O'Donnell immensely in developing trust among the Negros the two were about to encounter and Big George's *special sight* was invaluable for the long haul.

◆

Van Wyck had been a stop along the trading routes of early America. It was part of what was called the Waxhaw Township. Prominent churches were established there before the mid-1800s. The large mansions of the antebellum era survived the march of the Union troops through the South in the latter stages of the War Between the States.

The brick company there grew as the South's economy began to recover in the 1870s. Tommy Broome was a shrewd businessman who saw to it his company produced and sold the finest red clay brick around. The supply of cheap labor made for an ideal situation to help hold down costs. Many of the freedmen sought jobs there and small dwellings grew up near the brick yard. The recently constructed railroad passed nearby. It helped the business thrive all the more.

Thus, Van Wyck was an ideal location to start looking for the remnants of the lost time of slavery: those who might have been slaves at one time. Maybe there might be a certain former slave there O'Donnell had already met.

♦

"Big man, what are your thoughts?" O'Donnell asked George as they came upon the outskirts of the small village. "Where do you think we might start asking?"

"Boss man, it be's a good question," George replied. "Maybe we jus ride and look around for a whiles. We gots ta see where the peoples is. I speck any direction you wants to go is as good as the next."

"I guess ya'd be right big man. Let's go down this road; it looks worn to me. Might lead us to a good starting place," O'Donnell said with a smile.

O'Donnell was right. They had chosen the road which led to the brick yard and they could see there were many people at work and most of them were Black people.

"What say we go there and find out who's in charge and maybe if he can tell us anything about any of the people who work for him?" O'Donnell suggested.

Both nodded in agreement and they headed toward what they thought was the front of the building where they might find an office. Inside, they were greeted by a clerk who informed them Mr. Tommy, as he was called, was out in the yard.

Mr. Tommy was a character in his own right. He was talkative, jovial, and an all-around happy person. His happy-go-lucky personality never stopped him from being a good businessman who was always looking to sell the product he made. Actually, his personality was an asset to his ability to drive a good bargain.

O'Donnell and Big George decided to wait in the office after the clerk told them Mr. Tommy would return in a short while unless there were problems he needed to address right away.

"He always likes to spend time in the yard with the workers. He wants them to know he cares about them. They all work good, so he don't stand over none of 'em and make them work," the clerk also stated.

It wasn't too long until a bright-eyed smiling face came through one of the entrances to the yard and into the office. "What might I do for you gentlemen today? Have you got some special kind of brick in mind?" the forever salesman personality of Tommy Broome beamed.

"No, sir. We are here on a different matter, if you have a moment," O'Donnell politely said as he looked at Tommy.

"Well, I can take a moment. You gentlemen look like good fellas to me," Tommy replied. "What's this all about? My name is Tommy Broome and you gentlemen are?"

"This is George McAfee and I'm Thaddeus O'Donnell and we work for the railroad."

"So you gentlemen want to do some business for the railroad," Tommy blurted out.

"No, it's nothing of the sort. We've got kinda of an odd situation and we want to ask a favor of you if we might,"

O'Donnell said.

"I'm here to help you if I can," Tommy replied. "Just tell me how I might be of service."

"Well, sir, it's a fairly long story and if you have some time, I'd need to explain a portion of it so you'd know our concerns. You sure you have the time?" O'Donnell asked.

"Right now is fine. I'd be glad to give a listen," Tommy agreed.

"Well, it all started when we were doing some digging to lay the rail tracks up a ways east of here and we came across some bodies," O'Donnell started.

"Ah, so you're the ones who caused all the stir around here. My mama read about the bodies in the newspaper and said she even remembered when the man was hung. My mama, Mrs. Betty Broome, knows everything it seems," Tommy interrupted.

"Yes, sir, I'm afraid we are the ones who stirred up everything," O'Donnell started again.

"How might I or the brickyard be involved?" Tommy interrupted again.

"Well, sir, we came across a Negro who we feel might know a lot more about the original crimes than anyone who is still around," O'Donnell continued.

"You don't think one of my workers was involved in the crime, do you?" Tommy asked with a startled look on his face.

"We don't think the Negro we saw had anything to do with the actual crime, but he might have seen or heard something about it and we want to find out how much he might actually know. We believe he might be around these parts and we jus started here. He may not even be in the village. He may live another place. We thought we'd give it a try," O'Donnell said, finally without interruption.

"I bet mama would get a kick out of me knowing the two who found the bodies up at the old tavern after all these years. Tell you what, I'll take you out and let you look to see if you can identify the Negro you're looking for. You can tell if you see him, can't you?" Tommy asked. "But you will have to promise you will go with me to meet my mama. Mrs. Betty wouldn't rest if I didn't bring you by. No, she wouldn't be happy at all if she didn't meet you."

"We would be more than glad to visit your mother. But I would like to tell you it was my friend here who came across the bodies first. He was doing the work when they were dug up," O'Donnell said as a matter of clarity.

"I guess then we need to go out where they're working and see if we can spot your man. I have some workers who don't come in today. All of 'em don't work every day either, so you might have to come back tomorrow if you don't find your man," Tommy said courteously.

"If it won't disrupt anything, we may visit again if we have to. Are ye sure it's okay?" O'Donnell asked.

"You can come anytime you wish. Follow me and we'll go out and look around like you're here on business," Tommy instructed them as they headed toward a back exit into the work area.

♦

The three looked around the working areas for more than 45 minutes. Of course, part of it was Tommy's tour he normally gave customers. There was no one there who resembled the man O'Donnell had seen at the old inn and so the three finally left and went to see Tommy's mother for a pleasant visit.

♦

O'Donnell and Big George bid good day to the Broomes and decided to ride to another area before the sun sank too low.

"Big man, what's you thinking? Are ye thinking we are on a hopeless trail?" O'Donnell quizzed Big George.

"Cain't says I knows. I gots a feelins' we might be closer than we thinks. Yass, suh, I gots a feelin'," Big George surprisingly told O'Donnell.

"Big man, you sure you know what you feeling? I'm feeling if we are looking at a store just up the road, we ought to stop and get some supplies - if we intend to eat today," O'Donnell half laughingly said to George.

"You's rights, Boss Man, I thinks you's right," George replied.

Upon entering the old store, George was immediately attracted to a pretty Black female with a young boy who was paying for her small sack of goods.

O'Donnell playfully nudged George and said, "I can see what ye were feeling. I didn't know you could sense ladies, too."

George said nothing and showed his embarrassment with a grin.

As the lady turned and saw George face to face, each smiled at the other. George saw she was somewhat older than he had first thought. But in spite of her age, *she was still a striking beauty.*

O'Donnell and George continued about their

business of buying some needed supplies and walked out the door.

"Big man, you don't need be thinking about her. You'll have some man shoot you or cut you up over her," O'Donnell jokingly told Big George.

"Boss man, we both need to see her agin'," George said to a somewhat puzzled O'Donnell. "Boss man, she's the best looking woman I ever seed. Yass, suh, she'd make a man risk his life. Don't you thinks boss man?"

"It dawned on O'Donnell they just might have come across Chloe Jane. Both of them stopped short of mounting their horses as George said, "Boss man, we needs to ask the man inside who she be."

"Big man, we are headed back inside now!" O'Donnell said with an air of urgency.

"Pardon me, sir," O'Donnell said to the store proprietor as he approached the counter, "might you tell me about the lady who was just in here?"

"Mistah, you ain't the law, are you?" the proprietor asked.

"No, we are not associated with the law in any way. We're trying to find a friend who might be her husband," O'Donnell told the proprietor in a stern voice.

But still the skeptical storekeeper refused to give the name. "Mistah, I don't doubt you, but I ain't fond of telling who people is to strangers."

"Sir, we mean no harm to anyone. You need not worry," O'Donnell said in his best persuasive voice. "Mr. Tommy Broome will vouch for us."

"Then I speck you ask Mr. Tommy Broome about her husband," the storekeeper still defiantly stated.

"Good day, sir," O'Donnell said as he and George tipped their hats to the man. He knew he would not get any information from the clerk.

"Boss man," George started as they neared the horse, "she gots ta live round close to the sto. She had a youngin' wif her and it was pretty late in the day. We might oughta paid mo tention where she walked off to. I specks the youngin' was her grandchild. Theys all live bout here somewhere."

"I think ye right, big man. She won't be too hard to find. If she's Toney's wife or whatever he calls himself now, we'll find him. We might even try asking Tommy Broome tomorrow. But first, we need to find a place to camp, eat, and bed down for the night," O'Donnell said.

"I'm wif ya dere, boss man," a tired and hungry George replied.

◆

The fire was lit and George was cooking as O'Donnell rose from his knapsack. First order of business for the day was to go back to the brickyard and maybe, just maybe, Tommy Broome could tell them about the extraordinarily good-looking Black woman they had met at the store.

◆

But stranger things can happen. Just as they were approaching the brickyard, O'Donnell spotted a Black man off a ways from him who bore a strong resemblance to a man he had seen before. So he waited until the man had entered the working area and had gone to his work station.

"Good morning, gentlemen," came the greeting from Tommy Broome as O'Donnell and George walked into the office.

"Good morning to ye as well," O'Donnell said and he continued - wanting to get his questions in before Tommy Broome picked up a full head of speed with talk. "We have someone we'd like for you to tell us about if you don't mind. We saw a worker enter the gate today who we'd be real interested in talking with."

"Well, just point him out and we'll go talk to him," Tommy responded in a cooperative voice.

"Well, sir, we might want to have a long conversation with him in private," O'Donnell advised.

Tommy and O'Donnell walked out into the yard just close enough so as not to be noticed and O'Donnell nodded in the direction of whom he thought might be the man of interest. Tommy proceeded to get the man while O'Donnell went back into the office area.

When Tommy entered the room with the Black man and O'Donnell got an up close view, there was no doubt. This was the man who had talked to him along the road.

Tommy started, "This is Elijah and I told him you might want to talk with him."

When Elijah looked up and saw who had summoned him, he knew what it was all about.

♦

Could it be possible... Was some light about to be shed on the deep dark sinister happenings at the old tavern? Were the two railroad-builders, turned investigators, about to uncover some of the long held secrets of which only the ghosts of the travelers and the perpetrators of the dastardly crimes knew about?

CHAPTER TWENTY FIVE

Toney Tells the Truth
Late 1880s

"Elijah, haven't we met before?" O'Donnell starts, curious as to what reaction he would get.

"Yes, sirah... I reckon we has," came the reply.

"Last time we met was on a dirt road up in the Osceola area, I believe. You seemed to know something about what had happened there a long time ago, didn't you?" O'Donnell continued.

"Yes, sirah... I did," Elijah answered hesitantly.

"We're not here for the law. We're here because we want to know how the people we dug up were killed. We will assure you... no harm will come to you if you tell us what you know. We don't think you had anything to do with any of the killings and there's no one left around to do you and your family harm," O'Donnell said in an attempt to convince Elijah they were friendly. "I want you to answer this question truthfully. Mr. Tommy won't dismiss you if you tell the truth. Are you Toney?"

Elijah looked stunned. He could not believe anyone might ask him about being Toney. He looked for a way not to give a direct answer, but found none, and so he answered, "Yes, sirah... I guess the truths be knowed, I grew up Toney. I needed to change my name so nobody might find me. I thoughts maybe some of the peoples would come back looking fo me as longs as theys alive, fearin' I mights talk too much and theys gets in trouble."

"I don't think you need to worry anymore. I think you are still afraid of the law, and I promise he ain't gonna' harm you. Evidently, you wanted to get some of this off your chest or you might never have spoken to me on the road. Am I right?" O'Donnell asked is a sincere voice.

"Yes, sirah, I specks you done hit the nail on the head," Toney responded. "I guess I can tell alls I knows to you fokes."

"Mistahs, I swear for goodness I had nothing to do wif the axual killings and stealings. You gots to believe me. I had nothings to do wif it. I jes know whad I'd seed and whats I was told by my friend. Dats alls I knows, I promise!" Toney pleaded.

"Who told you about the killings?" O'Donnell quizzed as the usually talkative Tommy Broome looked on in amazement.

"My slave friend Matthew who was owned by Mr. Chaney. He done seed stuff he ought not seed and I speck they kilt him 'fore he sayed too much," Toney continued.

"What did your friend Matthew tell you?" O'Donnell asked. "How might you actually know Milt Chaney killed your friend? Do you think he might have sold him off to someone passing through?"

"Matthew done told me he knowed Mr. Milt was

stealing some. Matthew sayed Mr. Milt wadn't doing nothin' real bad. Then Matthew started telling me dat Mr. Milt was sneaking a slave ever now and then off to other places. He sayed he done telled them they'd gonna be freed. I thinks Matthew knowed better," Tony continued.

"So ye say your friend Matthew knew about Chaney stealing slaves?" O'Donnell responded.

"Thad be right. Matthew knowed about the slave stealing," Toney continued.

"Do ye know when the killing started?" O'Donnell quizzed Toney.

"I reckin I does. I won't swer exactly though. I knows Mr. Milt done been involved in stealing some things. Matthew never sayed anything 'bout no killing until a man wif a real fancy buggy and some fine horses done stayed at the inn one night. He sayed the man come back dere thinkin' he gonna get back his horse. Mr. Milt done kept it fo him til he got back and Mr. Milt done set a trap fo 'em. He sayed he thank dat be the first man Mr. Milt done kilt!" Toney continued emphatically.

"So ye think the man in the fancy coach was the first man Mr. Chaney killed?" O'Donnell asked.

"Matthew never sayed anything about him kiltin' nobody before he sayed he thought he'd done kilt the fancy man, sos I'm thinkin' he bees the first one," Toney said with some hesitancy.

"Well, how did ye know he was involved in killing others if your friend Matthew disappeared?" O'Donnell quizzed in a puzzled tone.

"I gots to wondering about what done happened to

my friend Matthew and starts sneakin' round and come upon some fresh dirt digging' and thoughts it might be Matthew's grave, but I specks I was wrong cause my 'nother friend sayed he knowed the men took Matthew off in a wagon. He mighta done had some of his peoples to take Matthew offs somewheres and kilt him!!" Tony said emphatically.

"Then... do you know how Chaney killed the people?" O'Donnell anxiously asked.

"Matthew sayed he done pisoned them," Tony replied as he shook his head.

"Then why did all the skulls have holes in them? The skulls looked like they had been hit with a hammer," O'Donnell pointedly asked, thinking of what George had said when he uncovered the first skulls.

"Matthew sayed Mr. Milt done made a hammer from part of an old anvil he done broke. He used it for lots of things. Matthew sayed he took the fokes after he pisoned them to the shed and to be sho they dead, he hits 'em all in the same place wif the hammer he done made. Matthew said he thought the first man he pisoned tried to wake up and so Mr. Milt got in a habit of jus' hittin' 'em anyhow!" Toney continues as the others shake their heads in disbelief that a man might be so cruel.

"Would certainly explain the holes in the skulls," O'Donnell said with a sigh. "Seems he got to enjoying the killin.'"

"Some people say Chaney had a wife and children. Did you know anything about them?" O'Donnell asks, hoping to find out more if possible.

"Matthew sayed and I fount out later, he had three chilren. He had a boy and two gir chilren. I thinks da boy was about eight or nine years old when dey hung his daddy. We was told what was left of his family went off to North Carolina," Tony said in somewhat of a certain voice.

"So you don't know exactly what happened to them after the hanging?" O'Donnell questioned even though he felt he would get no response.

"Well, sir, a funny thing I heared from some of my fokes who stayed over near where the plantation I left from. They sayed his boy growed up... and became a preacher man. Yes, sirah, a preacher man," Tony said with a slight snicker.

"Does sound a bit strange," O'Donnell said with a short chuckle.

All during this time, Tommy Broome and Big George have listened intently without so much as a question or remark of their own.

"Well, a couple more questions and I will let you go. Why did Chaney steal you and send you off to Virginia? Didn't he know you'd come back?" O'Donnell asked in a puzzled manner.

"Well, sirah, he done sent me off to be kilt. Dem fokes he sent me wif done tied me up and puts me in a wagon headed off to Virginie. Theys 'posed to kilt me along the way, but they sayed they'd sell me and get some money. They sayed they'd kilt me if'n I said a word. They sayed they'd kilt Chloe Jane too. Afters a while, I couldn't take no mo. I hads to git backs to where I was 'pose to be so's I tells de big man who had the plantation I was stolt, and where I was stolt from and who was responsible. He's didn't want to believe me so I rans aways and made it back. Well sirah... he came lookin' and got the sheriff and dats when the fokes around decided theys wants to hang Mr. Milt!" Tony once again states emphatically.

"It all makes sense now. Do ye have anything else ye haven't told us," O'Donnell queries.

"I speck I done tells you alls I knows," Toney said in an exhausted tone. "Yes, sirah, I done tells you all I can thinks about."

O'Donnell looks at Tommy Broome and nods to indicate he has finished with the questions.

"You can go back to work now, Elijah, or is it Toney? I want you to know I am proud of you and nothing is going to happen to you," Tommy said in a sincere voice to let Toney know he was safe.

"Much oblige, sirah, much oblige," Toney says in a relieved tone as he heads back to onlookers who feared he'd been fired or something worse. They can be seen shortly patting Toney, or Elijah, on the back.

"Boy, have I got a story to tell mama. This will make her happy for a long time. Yes, sir, the fact we finally know what happened at old Milt's tavern. To think I got the man working for me who knew what went on at Chaney's Inn. Boy, what a story I got to tell my mama!" Tommy repeated, hardly able to control himself. "I guess you fellas can rest now since you know what happened."

"Well, maybe not just yet," O'Donnell said to a puzzled Tommy Broome and Big George McAfee.

♦

Just what did O'Donnell have on his mind?

CHAPTER TWENTY SIX

The Box
Late 1880s

As they left the office of Tommy Broome, Big George got in front of O'Donnell and asked him pointedly, "Boss man, jus what you gots on yo mind? We gonna go tell the sheriff so's he can be happy and we can be done wif this?"

"Big George, we got some riding to do before this is over. I'm afraid we got a lot of riding to do, big man." O'Donnell responded.

"We gwanna go look for the preacher man, ain't we? Just what fo we gonna look fo him?" Big George questioned with a puzzled look.

"Big man, you always seem to have a hunch about things, and your hunches are good, but this time I feel a hunch of my own." O'Donnell responded once again.

"Boss man, they's lots of preachers and lots of places to go, and lots of ridin' and askin'," George said with a sigh.

"Big man, they said Milt Chaney was a big man with red hair. My hunch is we might be looking for a red-haired preacher. Don't you think we've narrowed it down some?" O'Donnell asked George.

"I reckon we has, if'n the man has red hair likes you say. Still gonna be lots of riding and askin' boss man. We sho nuff gonna be tired!" Big George countered.

Toney had been a store of information beyond belief. Little wonder Milt Chaney and the others had gone to such great pains to be sure he didn't talk. Not at all strange how the love of one beautiful woman had made him risk his life. He also must have been cunning enough to know once he committed himself to telling about being stolen from Dr. Crenshaw's plantation and sold off to another slave owner, Dr. Crenshaw would protect him and Chloe Jane. He had calculated correctly. No plantation owner would put up with slave stealing and once Milt Chaney was exposed, the rest of his gang would scatter. He would only need to worry about Steele and Steele had to lay low for fear he might eventually be hanged too.

♦

How hard it would be to find the red-haired Reverend was unknown. Toney's words were good, but they were still hearsay information. O'Donnell and George needed to stop in Waxhaw to water the horses and get some food for themselves as well.

They would ask anyone who looked like a churchgoer. They could ask anyone they thought might have some sort of answer and they did. They also rode for three days searching and there was no luck whatsoever. They had come across but one red-haired person of the age the preacher might be and he was not a native to the area.

"Big man, I think we maybe done failed on this mission," O'Donnell said with somewhat of a laugh.

"I spek you is right, boss man. Maybe we's go down and tell the sheriff all we's knows and then Ise supposing we gots to get back to railroad business," George responded.

"Big man, which one of these roads leads to Lancaster?" O'Donnell asked as they came upon a crossroads.

"Boss man, I thinks we gotta go back west and then go south if'n we gonnin' to see the sheriff in Lancaster," George said with some certainty in his voice.

"I think ye may be right, big man," O'Donnell said as nudged his horse in the chosen direction.

Neither of the two had any idea of how important the decision they just made would be.

Two miles down the road, they came upon another crossroads and visible behind a large cemetery was an antiquated church.

"Big man, do you think there's any use to look there?" O'Donnell asked with an almost exhausted voice.

"Boss man, you knows we gonna look, why you even ask?" George laughed.

"Ye right, big man. Don't think we'll have any luck, but we're gonna go up there anyway," O'Donnell said.

So the two went up the well-worn road to the church

building with a small dwelling near it, and as they got closer, they could see people doing chores in the yard.

"Good afternoon, ma'am," O'Donnell politely said as they neared the woman they saw working.

She gathered her two children around her and told one of them to go get his father. The child ran to the church.

"How are you gentlemen today?" she asked, somewhat startled and somewhat afraid because she did not recognize the men.

Just then, a robust man with reddish brown hair appeared from the area of the church and walked toward the men.

"How might I be of service to you gentlemen?" he asked sincerely.

"We were just passing through and needed to know which road we're supposed to be on to go to Lancaster," O'Donnell stated as George showed a puzzled look on his face about what O'Donnell had said.

"It would be the road you just came down. You'll need to go west for a few miles and then south when you see the next north/south road. Might I offer you gentlemen a drink of water? You both look a mite thirsty," the man said with a smile. "I'm Reverend John Helms and this is my wife Rebecca. These are our children, Jacob, Naomi, and Joshua."

"I'm Thaddeus O'Donnell and this is my trusted friend and co-worker George McAfee. We'd be glad to take ye up on the offer," O'Donnell responded. "We've got predty thirsty riding today."

The Reverend got a bucket of fresh well water and a dipper and handed it to the men.

"You folks not from around here, are you? What line

of work did you say you are in?" The Reverend prodded.

"We're in the railroad business," O'Donnell answered.

"Sounds interesting," came the reply from the Reverend who gave somewhat of a strange look as he answered.

"Much obliged for the water. We need to be on our way if we are gonna reach Lancaster before dark," O'Donnell said as he and George mounted their horses.

As they rode out of earshot from the family they had just met, Big George looked at O'Donnell and asked pointedly, "Boss man, why you didn't ask da man no questions? He looked like da man we'd lookin' fo."

"Didn't want to ask him questions in front of his family. In a strange sort of way, I think he knew what we were thar about," O'Donnell replied.

"I don't's gets it at all, boss man. We's rides all these days and we thinks we mights sees the man's we's after and you's don't talk to him at all!" George replied with a questioning look.

"Big man, let's get to Lancaster today so we can get some rest and give all of this more thought tomorrow," O'Donnell said with a half laugh as the two rode quietly the remainder of the way to Lancaster.

Some Coincidences are Planned?

Early the next morning, O'Donnell and George rode to the sheriff's office to speak with Sheriff Haile and inform him of what they had found out. Maybe the case could be closed and most who had taken an interest in it would be reasonably satisfied to know at least as much as O'Donnell and George knew. They felt they had started it, and they felt they had wrapped it all up. Well, somewhat.

"Good morning, gentlemen," the deputy said to O'Donnell and George as they entered the jail office, "What might I do for you today?"

"We'd like to talk with the sheriff if he's around," O'Donnell said.

"Well, I hate to tell you this, but the sheriff will be gone for a while. He might be back around noon or after," the deputy replied.

"Then we'll be back around then. The big man and I need to stock up on some supplies anyway. So we will see you then," O'Donnell said in a polite but somewhat disappointed manner.

◆

Noon was nigh and the two made their way again to the jail office. As they entered, they were greeted by the sheriff and, to their surprise, a Reverend Helms.

"Gentlemen, come in," Sheriff Haile smiled at O'Donnell and George. "Let's go back into the room here and talk a spell," he instructed. "Seems like this man has some information we might be interested in."

"This here is Reverend Helms," the Sheriff said with a grin to O'Donnell. "Reverend Helms, this is Thaddeus O'Donnell and his trusty sidekick, Big George McAfee."

O'Donnell and the reverend each extended their hands to one another and strangely, if for reasons of their own, neither let on they had previously met, which caused a huge puzzling frown on Big George's face.

They went to a room where the sheriff had taken O'Donnell and George before.

"Reverend Helms came to me in the last hour or so

and said he wanted to talk about what has been going on," Sheriff Haile continued. "Grab a seat and sit a spell."

As they sat, the Reverend took a small box from his coat pocket and placed it on the table.

"I guess this might be the best place to start. My mama gave this to me a long time ago and she said, 'Son, I want you to keep this. Someday you will know what to do with it. Well, I reckon the time has come. My daddy, and you fokes know who he was, gave this to my mama many years ago when I was just a young boy. He told her if something happened to him, she could use it to pay the taxes on the plot of land he owned. You know what happened to my daddy. Mama refused to pay the taxes with this and we lost the land. Mama was a good woman. She said she wasn't gonna use ill-gotten gain for any reason. She said some day it might go back to its rightful owner. Now, I don't know who the rightful owner was, but I want to give it to you, sheriff, because you might be able to find some of his relatives," Reverend Helms said apologetically.

The Reverend reached out and slid the box to the sheriff.

"Sheriff, I want you to find a relative of whoever this belongs to. I believe you will. I want to thank you gentlemen for your time. I want to tell you again my mama was a fine woman and don't judge her by what my daddy did. My daddy kept us all locked in the house after dark and whatever went on, we didn't know about. I just hope you believe me," Reverend Helms said sincerely.

"Sir," the sheriff started, "I believe you, I really do, and I think these men believe you. I just want you to know you did the right thing and I will forever be grateful. I believe I might know who this box belongs to."

With a nod, the good Reverend stood up, shook everyone's hand, tipped his hat, nodded to O'Donnell and Big George, and walked out the door.

The sheriff looked at O'Donnell and said, "Now, my deputy told me you had something to tell me. I'll bet you can't top what we was just told."

O'Donnell looked at George, both laughed slightly and O'Donnell said, "Sheriff, I think maybe you ought to sit back down."

CHAPTER TWENTY SEVEN

To Join Her Beloved John Mitchell
1890

Mrs. Alice DeMars had endured the hardships of the loss of her husband, the war, and all the many other things which might have broken a lesser woman. She had done so with grace. She maintained her strength through faith and believed in the end... all would be well. She was financially secure. Her husband's business thrived once again after the devastation of the war. Fate had also given her the precious gift of a good family which she spoke of often as she replayed the memories of her years on this earth. She sensed her days were nearing an end. Just as with all of life's other realities, she had accepted it with grace and had made her peace with those about her and most importantly, her Maker.

Her days were spent awakening later, moving around slower, and reflecting the past. She was still blessed with a clear mind and thoughts. She sat at times and stared out the windows as if to look for someone she knew would never return. Her eyes misted over, and then she recomposed herself, stood, and with the aid her cane, walked, looked, and checked certain things in the house. She still wanted her house to be well-kept and clean.

The visits from the children were more often and they

were quick to offer as much help as possible. Her first grandson John Carter was still her favorite. He had tried his best to fulfill her wishes and was still working on the last remaining wish she had – the promise of moving his grandfather's remains from Lancaster County to Camden and placing them in a proper grave.

♦

Carter looked up from his desk to see his mother Christie standing in front of him.

"Mother, you must forgive me. I was so involved in my work I didn't see you there," Carter said. "Is everything okay?" He noticed the look of deep concern on her face.

"Carter, your grandmother has had a stroke. We have called the doctor and he is in attendance. She is a gravely ill lady. The doctor is afraid her days are few," Christie told Carter in a depressed tone.

"I must go there immediately!" Carter exclaimed as he rose from his desk. "Do you have your carriage outside?"

"Yes, I do, but Carter, I don't think she will recognize you. Aunt Mimsie is there with her now. The doctor has given her only a slight chance to recover much at all. He said she needs as much rest as possible and we need to notify as many of the family as we can," Christie told Carter.

"Mother, I promised her so much and I feel as though I have failed on some of the most important things I promised – the things I promised her about grandfather," Carter said as the two left to go to the carriage.

They rode with only brief glances at one another as they held hands for comfort.

As soon as they arrived, Carter hastily went to his grandmother's bedside as she lay there unresponsive. He looked at her pleasantly with hope she might awaken to say one last goodbye, but she did not. Carter stood staring for more than an hour.

"Carter, your mother and I will stay with her," said Mimsie. "If you need to go back to the office, you should. There is nothing you can do here. The doctor thinks she's not ready to leave just yet. He said she has a strong will."

Carter hung his head as he left the room to make his way back to his office.

♦

Carter sat his desk for a lengthy time. He could not get the thoughts from his mind. He felt he had failed his grandmother badly.

It had been such a long time since his grandfather had disappeared. Carter was just a small boy at the time.

His mind drifted to the pleasant times when he had been initiated into the hunt with his grandfather and some of his grandfather's friends. He thought of the times of the Sunday meals at his grandparents' home and the other pleasurable moments he had spent there before his grandfather was snatched away.

He tried his best to concentrate on some of the work he needed to finish, but his thoughts of other things would not let go. He felt sad his grandmother would soon leave this earth never having known the details of what had happened to her beloved husband and thinking the two would not rest eternally by each other's side. There was nothing further he could possibly do in the short time she had left. He felt as though he had failed his most important mission in his life!

♦

Soon he heard a knock on his door. He stood up, sighed, and walked to the door, opened it, and was greeted by two men.

"Come in, gentlemen," Carter said. "What might I do for you today? I'm Carter Bradshaw. You'll have to excuse my disposition."

"I'm Matthew Shaw the Third and this is Ben Moore. We're from the Lancaster County Sheriff's office. We're here on some business. We were sent here personally by Sheriff Haile. We need to inquire about the belongings we have in this box. The sheriff felt real certain it belonged to you and he wanted you to have it as soon as possible."

One of the deputies handed Carter the box. Carter opened it and examined the contents. An incredulous smile appeared on his face as he said with a break in his voice, "Gentlemen, this belonged to my grandfather! How did you ever find it!?"

"Well, sir, it is a long story. The sheriff said he had promised to work with you and he thought we ought to bring this along with some information he wrote. He knowed you'd want to come back to Lancaster County as soon as you could. He said we still ought to bring this to you," Matthew said.

"You gentlemen don't know how much I appreciate this! I can never repay you enough. I will try to make it up to you. He's right. I have some rightfully important unfinished business up there," Carter said with renewed strength in his voice.

♦

After the two deputies had gone, Carter clutched the box tightly, let out a sigh of celebration, placed the box again on his desk, and opened the folder with papers the sheriff had sent. He hurriedly read with amazement what the sheriff had written. It was sketchy, but amazing. He knew he could get all the details first-hand when he returned to Lancaster and he knew now his return would be soon.

♦

First, he must rush to his grandmother's side once again and try to tell her what had been brought to him. He dashed from the office, boarded his buggy, and drove with haste to his grandmother's house. He briskly negotiated the steps. His mother noticed the clamor and greeted Carter at the door.

"There has been no change," his mother solemnly stated.

"I still must go see her!!" Carter said emphatically as he made his way to her bedroom.

Carter leaned over her bed, kissed his grandmother on the head, and whispered, "I love you grandmother. I just wish you could hear me."

Much to the astonishment of those who looked on, Mrs. Alice opened her eyes, even though it was a painful struggle.

"Grandmother, I have something for you!" Carter lovingly said. Trying his best to control his excitement mixed with other emotions, he took the box he had been given from his pocket. He gently placed the contents in his grandmother's frail hand. As he closed her fingers around the object, a faint smile appeared on her face. A small tear rolled down her withered cheek as she struggled to place her hand near her heart. Carter instinctively knew and gently guided her hand there.

With her last bit of energy, she glanced up at Carter, smiled again - this time as if all was well in the world. She slowly closed her eyes and drifted away.

Carter leaned forward again, kissed his grandmother on the forehead, straightened back up, turned, looked at his mother, and without comment or embrace walked quietly from the room.

EPILOGUE

Camden, South Carolina, is noted for its great history. Revolutionary War battles are commemorated there each year. Historical markers with names of Revolutionary War heroes are plentiful and their descendants take tremendous pride in ensuring their ancestors are honored to the fullest extent of their glory. Portraits of military leaders and heroes of the era adorn museums and private dwellings alike.

Black wrought iron fences surround cemeteries which hold remains dating back to the early 1700s. Marble monuments have aged with time and inscriptions are sometimes hard to read, but with a little effort, you can tell who is buried in the superbly maintained plots.

Just off to the edge from some of the more famous names, there is a lavish, but elegant marker which catches the beams of the early morning sun. Perfectly carved into the stone is the name of a *Mrs. Alice DeMars, b. 1801, d. 1890.* The inscription just below reads: *Beloved Wife of John M. DeMars.* Just beside it, and it might be hard to understand the inscription unless you know the story, reads: *John M. DeMars, b.1801, d.1852, Joined His Beloved Wife 1891.*

◆◆

How many families had Milt Chaney brought sorrow to? The truth can never be told on this earth. The history of the sordid tavern will never be fully known.

Was Chaney a man possessed by demons? Did he react to the forces of the full moon? Was there another answer for his sinister behavior?

Why would a man who seemed to be intelligent enough to have success at whatever he did resort to such vile behavior? The questions are many and the answers are few, and even then, only speculation.

◆◆◆

Oak trees made even more beautiful by the moss which adorns them surround the old forgotten cemetery. If any grave markers remain, they are unrecognizable. Off to one edge stands a fine granite marker inscribed: *James Hemmings, trusted friend. 1790 – 1852.* It is near the place where he witnessed his mother and father placed into the ground by the light of a torch when he was much younger. James was also laid to rest there, properly this time, by the light of the torch. Such a procession would have pleased him. Sheer coincidence or not, it was the second time he had been placed in a grave under a full moon.

◆◆◆

There's also a tale passed along from those who had been unfortunate enough to have ventured through the area of the old paupers' cemetery in Lancaster late at night. It goes something like this: *"If you go to the old graveyard where those who have been forgotten are buried, go there when the full moon is just overhead in the night sky, about three a.m. in the morning. Watch carefully as a knee deep mist rolls across the graves of the unknown travelers. Listen intently for a peculiar sound from a particular direction. Is it the sound of something heavy striking a blow? Listen still longer for a faint moan and continue your vigil and count the times the sounds are repeated. Do not cower and run; for you must look closely as soon as the next day dawns for a grave which will be indented unlike it was the day before. Tell no one to 'come back to look at the site,' for none will believe you. The marks will have disappeared by the time you return. Be careful if you go there."*

ADDENDUM

The book, as stated, was a mixture of fact and fiction. What follows below is a factual account by Louise Pettus about Milt Caney and the disposition of his property after his death. I would like to add to this: Lindsay Pettus, Louise's brother and local Historian Extraordinaire in his own right, told me in a discussion - Milt Chaney's widow eventually moved back to Virginia. It is thought Milt Chaney was originally from Virginia.

Chaney/Cheyney
Pettus
DARK DOINGS AT CHANEY'S TAVERN

Milt Chaney's trial, held in the courthouse in Lancaster in March of 1856, was a sensation. People still wonder if the bearded giant stashed away gold in the area around the tavern.

The tavern, located in the northeastern corner of the junction of today's Highway 521 and Highway 75 in the

Indian Land section, catered to weary travelers between Camden and Charlotte – and points beyond. Too often, it was the last known place the traveler stopped.

When relatives who were missing their husband, father, or son, who was returning home after selling livestock, a slave, bales of cotton, or other goods, traced the route taken by the missing man, they usually ended up pointing a finger of suspicion at Chaney.

For years the story has been told in which Chaney killed his victims with an anvil he hoisted to the ceiling and dropped. Some say the anvil hung in the dining room and others say it hung in the bedroom. The story probably has no basis. However, a few years ago, ago some gold searchers using a Geiger counter dug up an old anvil.

Chaney's trial, though, centered on another matter. He was charged with "Negro stealing." Specifically, Chaney was charged with stealing Toney from the plantation of Dr. R. L. Crawford, taking him to Virginia and selling Toney as if he were his own. Years after Toney was kidnapped, the sheriff of King William County, Virginia, contacted the Lancaster County sheriff to help him recover the money a Mr. Powell had paid for Toney. It seems Toney had told his story to the sheriff in the hope of being sent back to the Crawford plantation in Lancaster District.

Toney's story only confirmed the old belief Chaney was a part of an organized gang who kidnapped slaves to sell out of state after enticing the slaves with promises of helping them reach freedom in the North. John M. Steele, a neighbor, was the chief witness for the state. All of the evidence against Chaney was damning and he was found guilty.

Chaney appealed the verdict and for a time was lodged in the Richland County jail. The appeal failed and Chaney was sent back to Lancaster to be hanged.

The people believed Chaney would confess and implicate his co-conspirators. He never did. Instead, "calm and cool" for an hour and a half, Chaney addressed the crowd gathered for the hanging. He ignored shouted pleas for him to confess.

Later, a poem Chaney penned in his cell was made public. The poem was addressed to Chaney's 26-year-old wife who was listed in the 1850 census only as "P. Chaney." The poem began:
"My days are numbered they are but few
When I must bid this world adieu.
Dear wife, how happy I could be
If your dear face I could see..."

Chaney, according to a *Lancaster Ledger* account, had three children at the time of his trial. If so, they were all under 6 years. The 1850 census listed only a 12-year-old boy, J. Vicory, in his household. In his poem, Chaney wrote, "Dear infants, I bid you farewell, My love for you no tongue can tell...."

Chaney wrote of his in-laws, referring to his mother-in-law as: "all the friend your father had. Her weeping eyes you often see, Is wet with tears and all for me...."

On July 11, 1856, in front of a large crowd outside the Robert Mills designed jail, Milton M. Chaney was hanged. The last lines of his poem were:
"On earth no longer I can stay
Because my life was sworn away.
His name, it's true, I can't conceal,

It was the one-eyed John Steele."

Many years later when Highway 25 to Waxhaw, N.C. was being hard-surfaced, construction workers found numerous skeletons close by Chaney's Tavern.

Records of Court Proceedings

1856-Lancaster Book R, 307. J. D. Haile, sheriff

Heath, M. C.

.goods, chattels, lands or tenements of J (?) or I Gallachat to levy the sum of $53.00 - all of Gallichat interest in and to fifty acres of land M. O. I. Known as the homestead formerly belonging to Milton M. Chaney (dec'd), bounded by land of M. C. Heath, Allen Morrow and others. $75.00 bid by M. C. Heath, highest bid.

In the presence of

M. L. Belk

J. A. Stewman

1856 - Lancaster Book R, 308:

M. C. Heath:

Writ of Fieri Facias issued out of the Court of Common Pleas; suit of John Crockett, Adm. . . . . all the goods and chattels, land, etc. of Milton M. Chaney to levy the sum of one hundred twenty one and 24/00 - I, J. D. Haile seized and took of the land and tenements of the said Milton M. Chaney all his interest in and to 50 acres of land known as the homestead bounded by land of M. C. Heath, Allen Morrow and others, for the sum of $25.00, being the highest bidder thereof.

1862, Lancaster Book S, p. 336.

I, R. C. Potts, one of the notary publics for said district do hereby certify to all whom it may concern: Faetnah

Little formerly the wife of Milton M. Chaney, dec'd, this day appeared before me and upon being privately and separately examined by me did declare she does fully voluntarily and without any compulsion dread or fear of any person or persons whomsoever, Renounce, Release, and forever Relinquish unto Moses C. Heath his heirs and assigns, all of her interest and estate, also all of her right and claim of dower in or to a certain tract or parcel of Land Situate and being in the district aforesaid on the waters of Twelve Mile Creek bounded by lands of M. C. Heath, Allen Morrow and James Delany. Said land is known as the Home Sted of the said Milton M. Chaney, dec'd.

Given under my hand and seal this the 8th Oct 1862
Phetnah Little
(Seal) R. C. Potts, N. P.
Recorded 2nd January 1862 (by) H. J. Hancock

ABOUT THE AUTHOR

Don L. McCorkle

The author grew up in the panhandle area of Lancaster County, SC, and graduated in 1962 from, what was then, a small rural school named Indian Land. Starting in the 1980s, the area experienced some of the most rapid growth in the state,

Don's formal education included graduating from North Greenville College, Newberry College, and Winthrop University. He earned degrees in

History/Political Science and Psychology and post graduate degrees in Education Administration. His career as a high school teacher in Chester County, SC, teaching Psychology, History, and other related subjects lasted 31 years.

He served in the U.S. Army, active duty, for three years. One year of his service, 1968-69, was spent as an Automatic Weapons Platoon Leader in Vietnam. He received a Bronze Star for his service during his tour of duty there.

An enlistment option called "The Buddy Plan" allowed him and his high school friend to endure basic combat training together. The same friend, Jacky Bayne, was gravely injured in Vietnam when his scout dog triggered a personnel mine. Jacky was actually given up for dead twice until graves registration specialists discovered he was alive.

The Buddy Plan is another completed book, not yet published, which chronicals Jacky's amazing life since the fateful day of his misfortune. The book also tells additional amazing true stories about other veterans.

Don has a third book in the works titled *Diaries in the Drawer*. A lady discovers two diaries inadvertantly left in an old piece of furniture at an antique store. The woman is a mature lady with a young inquisitive mind. For some reason, destiny has chosen her for the task of solving the complex mystery.

The author has retired and moved back to the area where he grew up in Indian Land, SC.

www.ingramcontent.com/pod-product-compliance
Lightning Source LLC
Chambersburg PA
CBHW072106170626
46813CB00004B/1474